STUCK
IN THE LAND
OF THE
PHARAOHS

DAVE JOHNSON

Cover art by Jessica Bell

ISBN: 9781739132651

In memory of my mother, Joan Johnson. She appeared in my first book as Joan the Land Army Girl, and she passed away while I was writing this one.

The Stuck Series

1, Stuck in Time.

2, Stuck 1595: An Elizabethan Adventure.

3, Stuck 1824: A London Tale.

4, Stuck 1855: Lucy Travels East.

5, Stuck 1966: No Time To Groove.

6, Stuck in the Land of the Pharaohs.

7, Stuck Between Two Lives

All books are stand-alone stories

CHAPTER ONE

Archie Baxter polished every inch of Big Bessie with a soft, dry cloth. Perhaps not such a strange thing to do when you consider that Big Bessie was a time machine, not a person. On the other hand, most people would think it strange to own a time machine in the first place. Archie didn't just own it, he had built it from scratch, and the only other people that knew about Big Bessie were Robert, James and Lucy Baxter. Not even his housekeeper, Mrs Simpson, knew that in Archie's dusty ground-floor office in his private Cambridge museum, a hidden switch activated a sliding door that revealed his secret lab.

You couldn't really say that thirteen-year-old twins Robert and James, and their twelve-year-old sister, Lucy spent most of their time at Greystones Boarding School in Anchester. Their friends thought they did, but every now and then, they were summoned to meet their Uncle Archie and, as a result, could spend months in another time and another place and still be back at school before anyone noticed. The existence of Big Bessie wasn't the only family secret. All the Baxter children had suffered from a mysterious condition that had turned them invisible at one time or another. Not only was this extremely inconvenient, to say the least, but it was also a condition that, if not dealt with, could be fatal. The key to their health and wellbeing was Big Bessie.

Everything was linked. Archie had incorporated both his DNA and that of the children's parents into Big Bessie's software when he created the time machine. The children's parents had been explorers and had gone missing years before, but Big Bessie recognised the DNA passed on to Robert, James and Lucy. Big Bessie and the museum were also linked; the machine's data contained the catalogue of all the exhibits and occasionally would identify when something was missing. Archie had refined the software so that sometimes Big Bessie could predict that one of the children would shortly become invisible. She would provide them with the solution, which was always to find an item from the past and to enter it into the museum catalogue via the 3D scanner. The problem was that the clues she gave were usually rather vague, and invariably the children set off back in time with no idea what they were looking for.

Archie hummed an old pop song as he polished. The 1970s was the era when he was rising through the ranks of the army, eventually ending up in a top-secret job, but he was an old hippy at heart and had a passion for 1960s and 1970s music. Maybe these two diverse aspects of his character had led him to think outside the box and given him the self-belief to think that time travel might be possible. However, his understanding of the military made him realise that Big Bessie's existence and the condition that rendered the Baxter children invisible had to remain a secret. Invisible time-travelling soldiers? It was his worst nightmare!

Archie always polished Big Bessie in the same sequence. He started at the end with the large flatbed scanner, checked the vacuum pump was attached correctly, and cleaned the chrome levers and catches. Then he moved on to the bank of computer hard drives that rose almost to the ceiling. He always left Big Bessie switched on, so as he dusted, dozens of little LED lights appeared to wink at him. He knew it was silly, but Archie liked to wink back. After that, he came to the cabinet with slots for the wooden blocks that operated the machine. Archie stored more of these blocks in drawers at the bottom of the time machine. They had metal bases and were inscribed with letters from the runic alphabet. His code-writing skills came into play here because he used them to programme Big Bessie when transporting Robert, James, Lucy and himself. It was Lucy who had cracked the code when she and the twins had first discovered the lab, after Archie had managed to get stuck in 1940.

Finally, Archie polished the glass screen. It was connected to Big Bessie by a brightly-coloured coil of electrical wire. Behind it was the window seat where the Baxters would sit to be transported to another time and place. Archie regretted that, on so many occasions, the burden had been on Robert, James and Lucy to travel back in time and face seemingly insurmountable problems. However, so far, the children had always managed to achieve success by working together as a team. On the occasions when Archie made an attempt to find the items that Big Bessie had identified by himself, it had always ended in failure.

With the screen finished, Archie stepped back to admire his work. Big Bessie was gleaming. The sound of her computers whirring away made it seem as though she were purring with content. He had timed it just right. Mrs Simpson, his housekeeper, would be setting his meal out on the table in a few moments, before returning to her apartment on the top floor. Archie failed to see two things as he shut the secret door to the lab behind him. Big Bessie's monitor screen flickered into life. It displayed the message, 'Warning, advance notice of impending catalogue issue' and, on the ceiling above Big Bessie, was a small brown stain that hadn't been there the day before.

CHAPTER TWO

Lucy was fighting to stop her emotions from showing. She had gone for her tutorial with her new art teacher Henri Pastiche full of confidence, but now she struggled to hold back the tears. On the table in front of her was her latest assignment. It was a copy of one of her favourite paintings, "Going to the Match", by LS Lowry. Both of her brothers had seen it and were full of praise.

'You would never know it wasn't the original,' James had said. Robert, too, had complimented her. Perhaps its sporting subject had influenced him - you could describe Robert as being 'sports mad' - but he genuinely seemed to like it. Lucy herself had been proud of it. She felt she had captured the mood of the original painting with its crowd of figures heading towards a football stadium in a northern industrial city.

However, her teacher wasn't at all impressed.

'Lucy, Lucy, Lucy,' he intoned, shaking his head as he spoke. 'It's just copying. Yes, I can see skill with the paintbrush, and you have an eye for colour, but I want to see originality. Where is the spirit? You must strive to produce art that will live on long after you have gone. A copy! Where is the value in that?' He leapt to his feet and spent the rest of the tutorial pointing at various posters on the walls and extolling the virtues of the artists who had painted them.

'See! See! This Hockney. Do you see what I mean? He has it. Oh yes, he has it....'

As Henri Pastiche paced around the room, seemingly excited by the sound of his own voice, Lucy concluded that she did not much care for Monsieur Pastiche. Luckily, he was only a temporary teacher, at Greystones Boarding School for just one term, so she would not have to put up with him for too long. It was not just the fact that he didn't like her painting that she found upsetting; Henri Pastiche seemed oblivious to her feelings. The more she focussed on what she didn't like about her teacher, like the ridiculous bow tie he wore or how his hair curled over his collar, the easier she found it possible to mask her feelings.

'So make your mark in history,' he said as he handed back her painting. Lucy nodded and strode out of the Art Room, holding her head up high.

***

James' audition at Drama Club was not going smoothly either. Perhaps his school-wide reputation for being a good actor had given him an inflated view of his abilities. He certainly hadn't prepared very well for this occasion, assuming he could wing it as he usually did.

'What kind of accent do you call that?' demanded his teacher, 'And you can wipe that smile off your face, my boy. It's not supposed to be a comedy, although, quite frankly, your acting is a joke! I've heard enough! Go away and put some serious work into this. Next time, if there isn't any improvement, you'll be lucky to get a job as an usher for the next production!'

***

Robert's problem was more physical than emotional. His coach expected him to win this race, but every other runner on the track had passed him by now. Clutching his side, he slowed to a walking pace. He grimaced, as he crossed the finishing line and called out to his teacher, Mr Hibbs:

'Sorry, coach. Stitch.'

'Self-inflicted,' replied Mr Hibbs, hands on his hips and clearly annoyed.

'How do you mean? It just came on by itself,' protested Robert.

'I was in the dining room and noticed that you went up for a second helping of steak pie.'

'Yes, well…' Robert's voice trailed off; he thought he had better keep quiet about the extra portion of pudding that he had wolfed down.

'And what did I see you drinking just before the race?' continued Mr Hibbs.

'Just my sports drink.'

'Exactly! Sugary sports drinks are known to cause problems like this just before a race. You should be drinking water and watching your diet. If you want the school to enter you into the regional trials, then you had better get your act together.' Mr Hibbs turned and strode away, leaving Robert standing dejected because deep down, he knew his coach was right.

***

At the same time of day, but over a hundred years earlier, Archie Baxter was having a more successful time. It was his twentieth visit of the day to the Burlington Fine Arts Club in Savile Row, courtesy of Big Bessie. He had only been away from the lab for twenty minutes, but he had spent several hours in the club on each visit over a period of months. He had one express purpose: to befriend George Herbert, better known as Lord Carnarvon, and that plan was working.

'Baxter, my good man!' hailed Carnarvon from across the room. 'Come and join us.' Archie raised his glass in salute and walked over to the party lounging on leather sofas near a window. As he walked, he swirled his drink, so the ice clinked against the side of the glass. On his first visit, Archie had had a quiet word with the barman so that whenever he ordered 'the usual', he would be given a drink that looked like a gin and tonic but contained no alcohol. Archie felt he could trust the barman to keep his secret. He didn't usually have a problem drinking alcohol. It was just that if he had tried to drink twenty gin and tonics in as many real-time minutes, he would have been very, very drunk by now.

Befriending Lord Carnarvon had been surprisingly easy because they shared a passion for motor cars.

'I was reading about you earlier today,' chuckled Archie as he slumped down on the sofa. He was actually feeling quite tired. A full day of time travel was beginning to take it out of him.

'Really?' said Lord Carnarvon, giving Archie a wink, 'Nothing too complimentary, I hope. I have my reputation to think about.'

'No, far from it. My good friend Bertie Glugle gave me an old newspaper cutting from about twenty years ago. You had to go before a judge. What did it say now? You were driving at terrifying speeds of up to twenty-five miles per hour and frightening pedestrians.'

'Hah! I remember it!' laughed Lord Carnarvon. 'The police constable was particularly peeved because I didn't stop when he put his hand up. How could I? My racehorse was running in the two-fifteen at Newmarket. I couldn't be late for that. Actually, if you ever need a good barrister, I'd recommend Staple Firth. He's a motorist's friend; he got the charges thrown out of court.'

'Haha! I might need him if I ever drive at the terrifying speed of twenty-five miles per hour. Seriously though, what is the current land speed record?'

'It's still a hundred and twenty-five miles per hour, set by Lydston Hornsted back in 1914. Mind you, on a good day, my 1912 Bugatti can reach ninety-nine miles per hour!'

'Fabulous car,' replied Archie with genuine enthusiasm. However, he kept to himself the fact that Big Bessie had sent him sixty-five miles, from Cambridge to London, in a fraction of a second, not to mention the journey of a hundred years back in time!

'So what about joining me this winter as transport manager for the season?' asked Lord Carnarvon. Archie nodded enthusiastically. This conversation was progressing just the way he hoped it would.

'It would be an honour and a pleasure,' replied Archie. 'I know you mentioned payment, but that won't be necessary. Just living expenses, and I can make my own way there. Actually, I will have to bring along three youngsters, my nephews and niece, Robert, James and Lucy, but they will be no trouble at all.'

'Excellent,' said Carnarvon, thrusting out a hand, 'Let's shake on it. Now, one more for the road? Have I introduced you to Howard here?'

'No, I don't believe you have,' said Archie, reaching out to shake hands with a thick-set man in his forties sporting a bushy moustache. 'I know of you, of course.'

'Yes, you do look familiar, but I don't believe we have spoken,' said Howard. Archie nodded in agreement, although he knew Howard was quite wrong. Archie had spoken to him the day before; only the date had been in 1895. It was in this very same club, at a photography exhibition. Archie had tried to strike up a conversation but found it quite challenging to make any headway. At that time, Howard had a reputation as a gifted watercolour artist, but Archie had found him rather earnest and solitary, and he hadn't found a way to make a connection. That was why he had then turned his attention in the direction of the more sociable Lord Carnarvon.

Thirty minutes later, with dates and addresses written in his notebook, Archie said goodbye to his new friends.

'Sorry old chaps; must fly! I have a long way to go.' Actually, all he had to do was pop into the club's library, stand behind the far bookshelf, and wait for Big Bessie to collect him. After that, Archie had two more tasks to do. He had to send texts to Robert, James and Lucy, and he had to phone through to Georgio's and order pizzas.

***

Robert, James and Lucy sat around the big table in their Uncle's secret lab. They all had mixed emotions. None of them had had a particularly rewarding day at school and they were thankful for any distraction. However, receiving a text telling them that their Uncle Archie had primed Big

Bessie to bring them back to Cambridge was usually a sign that there was trouble afoot. On the other hand, there were four different varieties of pizza on the table.

'Live for the moment,' thought James to himself as he reached out and took a slice of pizza. Robert had resolved to eat a little less than he usually would but then decided that his new, healthy eating regime could wait another day. Lucy, as usual, was a paragon of self-control and didn't follow the example of her brothers.

Archie knew that the critical information he needed to share had to wait until all the pizza had disappeared. Finally, the Baxter children finished eating and looked towards their Uncle.

'I guess that Big Bessie has been whispering something in your ear,' said James.

'You guess correctly, my boy,' replied Archie. 'She displayed the error message that indicates one of you three may become invisible unless we take action.'

'And did Big Bessie tell you where we have to travel to, and what year it will be?' asked Lucy.

'Er, not exactly,' replied Archie, shaking his head.

'No surprises there then,' said Robert.

'In fact,' continued Archie, 'All I have are three letters…T…U…T.'

'Oh, tut, tut Big Bessie. Is that the best you can do?' sighed James.

'I think you have to look way back in history,' said Archie, 'Tutankhamun.'

'Toot and come in! Is that some kind of historical doorbell?' laughed James.

'Shut up, James,' said Lucy. Hardly a day would go by without her saying those three words to curb the flights of fancy that James' imagination would take.

'Honestly, it's a foreign language to me too,' said Robert.

'Funny you should say that, because there is something else about Big Bessie that I must tell you,' said Archie. 'For now, let's deal with the matter in hand. Lucy, I imagine that you know what, or rather who, I'm talking about.'

'Yes, Uncle. He was an Egyptian Pharaoh. The boy-king.'

'Ah! Now you're talking. I think I would make rather a good boy-king. First of all, I would…' Lucy silenced James by giving him 'one of those looks' together with a warning in the form of a long-drawn-out:

'Jaaames!'

With James now silent, although not entirely serious because he had pinched his lips shut between his finger and thumb, Archie continued:

'I have been very busy since I got Big Bessie's warning yesterday. There were two important figures associated with the discovery of King Tut's tomb; the man who discovered it, Howard Carter, and his backer, Lord Carnarvon. As it happens, I've met them both; I have become quite pally with Herbie and, what's more, he's invited us to stay.'

'Herbie?'

'His full name is George Herbert, 5th Earl of Carnarvon, but we are…'

'Mates,' said Robert. 'When are we going?'

'If you mean, what time are we going, it's tonight. If you mean on what date will you arrive, the answer is 1922.'

'Tonight?' exclaimed Lucy in surprise. 'Where are we going?'

'Egypt. Don't worry, I know you will need some sleep, but it won't take Big Bessie long to get us there and I have a hotel booked. We can take a few days to get acclimatised, but then I will have work to do. I'm Herbie's transport manager.'

'Erm! Slight worry,' said Robert, 'My Egyptian is rather lacking, in fact it's non-existent. I only know the name of one Egyptian footballer. Every Egyptian knows his name. Fabulous player, you should see him…'

'Very useful,' interrupted Lucy drily, 'Given that he won't be born until seventy or eighty years after we get there. Robert does have a point though, Uncle. None of us speaks Egyptian. Can we succeed by only talking to English people?'

'Ah, that's the other thing I wanted to talk about,' said Archie excitedly. 'I've been updating Big Bessie, and I've introduced something I call the transcoder. I've tested it out. I've got a smattering of foreign languages under my belt from my time in the army, but I'm not fluent in any of them. However, now that I've activated the transcoder, I speak just like a local and understand everything wherever I travel to. If it works for me, given that my DNA is built into Big Bessie's code, then, fellow Baxters, I'm hoping it works for you too!'

It was as if Big Bessie were listening because suddenly she whirred into life and her printer slowly chugged out a message, "remember sunscreen."

'Thank you, Big Bessie.' said Robert, giving the time machine a double thumbs-up gesture but raising his eyebrows in exasperation, 'You're always soooo helpful.'

'Now, now!' admonished Archie, 'If it wasn't for Big Bessie, just think where you would be.'

'In my dorm at school watching a movie on TV, not stuck in an Egyptian desert,' suggested James. Then he laughed, 'I know we all appreciate what you and Big Bessie do for us, Uncle, it's just that if she told us exactly what to bring back, life would be a lot easier.'

'Where exactly are we going to, Uncle?' asked Lucy.

'First stop is the city of Luxor, once the ancient city of Thebes. To be precise, Big Bessie is taking us to the ancient temple of Amun-Ra. Hopefully, most of the tourists will have gone, but we'll still be able to get a taxi ride to our hotel. So, my good people, if you would be so kind as to take your seats behind the glass screen, Big Bessie will take us back to October 1922.'

CHAPTER THREE

Robert, James and Lucy gazed in stunned silence as they circled on the spot. They were standing in the ruins of a magnificent, ancient temple. Carved stone pillars soared above their heads. Enormous stone statues stood guard along a passageway that stretched as far as they could see.

'Come along,' urged Archie. 'This is Karnak. You'll get the chance to come back and see it another day; it's been here for about five thousand years, so I'm sure it will wait for you. We've got to go and find a bus or a taxi.'

'James! What are you doing?' cried Lucy, in that voice that made it very clear that she disapproved. James was walking sideways with his head turned to look in the direction he was going, one hand held up close to his shoulder, the other out straight in front of him.

'I'm walking like an Egyptian,' replied James. 'I want to blend in.'

'Well, you don't. You look stupid!'

'Come along,' repeated Archie, and all four of them settled into a steady pace trying to catch up with some people they could see in the distance. It was a sweltering, dusty walk. Heat radiated from the buildings and appeared to shimmer before them. They continued along an avenue, lined with carved stone sphinxes, the bodies of lions with the heads of humans, which watched their slow progress.

'Mistake!' said Archie, 'It's the end of the afternoon; I didn't expect it to be this hot. I should have thought to bring some water to drink. Hopefully, it's not far now.' They came to a colossal statue.

'That's one of the Pharaohs, Ramses II, I think,' said Archie.

'Yes, it is,' agreed Lucy, 'I looked him up before leaving the lab.'

'You would,' muttered Robert. Lucy didn't rise to the bait; it was too hot to quarrel with her brothers.

By the time the Baxters reached the outer edge of the temple complex, most of the other tourists were already on their way to the city, although there were still a few people trying to negotiate the fare for the taxi ride to their hotels.

Robert moved closer to where several taxi drivers were chatting with each other. After a while, he returned to the other Baxters, a big smile on his face.

'Your new translating app is working well, Uncle,' he said,' I could understand the taxi drivers' conversations. They were joking, reckoning they could charge that party of German tourists treble the correct fare. For some reason, they think we will only pay double the fare.'

'Thank you for that,' chuckled Archie, 'I think that we

had better keep quiet about being able to understand Egyptian. It might prove to be very useful. You said there are German tourists. Could you understand them too?'

'Hmmm!' replied Robert, wiggling his hand in a 'so-so' gesture, 'I kind of got the gist of it. Not like with the Egyptians, they were as clear as anything.'

'Make the most of it, my boy; once Big Bessie takes you back home, I'm afraid you will have lost this new ability,' said Archie. 'Now, let's negotiate a fair rate for our ride to the Winter Palace Hotel.'

The taxi pulled away. The driver wasn't the most cheerful of souls, probably because he was only going to get a fraction of the money he had hoped for to cover the ten-minute journey to the hotel.

'If you look to your right,' said Archie, 'You will see the River Nile.'

'My! It's massive,' exclaimed Lucy.

'It certainly is,' replied Archie, 'It's over two miles wide just here. It's fantastically important to Egypt. Everything revolves around it. When it floods, as it does every year, it fertilises the soil. Actually, it doesn't flood so often in our own time because they built the Aswan Dam in the 1960s; since then, the farmers have had to use chemical fertilisers. Oh, look! We're here.'

'Wow!' the three children chorused in unison. Archie smiled.

'Yes, it is rather impressive, isn't it. Nothing but the best for the Baxters.' Before them, facing the river, stretched a long, three-storey building that wouldn't have looked out of place in any European city. The imposing sand-coloured facade, with its large windows and decorative balconies, cast deep shadows as it caught the last of the evening sun. A staircase curved around to the first-floor entrance, where a large portico completed the grand effect.

'Apart from the fact that royalty stay here, this hotel has another claim to fame. You've heard of the writer, Agatha Christie, I presume?

'Didn't she write 'Death on the Nile'?' asked Lucy.

'I saw the film,' chipped in James.

'Well, in about fourteen years, she will be writing the book in this hotel.' All four Baxters jumped out of the taxi and Archie paid the driver. As Lucy turned to close the door, she heard the driver mutter something.

'Uncle, why did the taxi driver say 'Imperialist dogs' under his breath,' she asked.

'Ah! That will be because political negotiations are happening at the moment. Right now, in 1922, Egypt is part of the British Empire, but later this year, it will gain its independence. Britain is reluctant to relinquish control over the Suez Canal, which passes through Egypt and links the Mediterranean and the Red Sea. It won't let go for another thirty years or so until it is forced to by the Egyptians. I'm afraid we are in a time when Britain felt it had the right to rule the world. So, we must be discreet. No politics, and of course, don't let on that King Tut will be discovered later this year. Anyway, let's check in.'

The Baxters, unencumbered by luggage, climbed the stairs leading to the hotel entrance. In true Baxter fashion, Robert sprinted to the top, determined to be first, jumped up in the air and spun around, commencing to shadow box, 'Rocky-style'. Meanwhile, Lucy climbed the steps steadily and demurely, unlike James, who had decided that he was the reincarnation of Fred Astaire and was attempting to tap dance up them. Archie, bringing up the rear, huffed and puffed as he hauled his rather overweight body up to the entrance. He paused a few moments to get his breath back, then they all entered the hotel and walked through a room that resembled a ballroom more than a hotel lobby.

Archie walked up to the reception desk.

'Hello, we are the Baxters. I'm Archibald... Archie, and I do believe Lord Carnarvon has booked some rooms for us.'

'Ah yes, Lord Carnarvon has been coming here for nearly twenty years now. I do believe we are his favourite hotel. The porter will take you to your suite. You have no luggage?'

'No, no. We're travelling light. Perhaps you could arrange for some clothes to be brought to the hotel for us.'

'Certainly, Sir. Enjoy your stay.'

CHAPTER FOUR

Archie had work to do. He had to spend the morning organising the transport for Howard Carter's archaeological expedition. There was a car for sale in Luxor that Archie wanted to inspect. He also wanted to check on the Model T Ford that Lord Carnarvon stored in one of the tombs, on the other side of the Nile.

'In a tomb?' laughed James, 'Won't it be all dirty, and can you only drive it at night as you rise out of the graveyard, followed by hordes of zombies, all shuffling along sideways and …?'

'James!' warned Lucy.

'No,' chuckled Archie, 'Across the other side of the Nile is the Valley of the Kings and three thousand years ago, when this city was called Thebes, the Egyptians cut long tunnels into the side of the mountain to bury Pharaohs and other important people. The car's in one of the empty tunnels. I need to see if I can get it running. It means I will be away all this morning. Can you amuse yourselves?'

'Yes,' Lucy reassured him, 'We can go for a nice leisurely walk.'

***

When Robert, James and Lucy were returning to the hotel after exploring the surrounding area, they heard music.

'I recognise that tune,' said Lucy, 'It's "The British Grenadiers". It sounds like a military band is playing in that park near the hotel. We have to go that way anyway, so come on, let's go and see.'

'Yes Sir, straight away, Sir, quick march,' replied James, saluting Lucy and marching away at double speed, his arms swinging in an exaggerated fashion. Meanwhile, Robert started running on the spot, then, keeping this action going, moved forwards to trot alongside Lucy. She shook her head, both exasperated and amused at the predictability of her brothers.

The three Baxters entered the park and now, as well as the sound of the military band, they could hear shouting. Ahead of them, they saw the red coats and tall furry black hats of the musicians as they marched towards them, determined to finish the tune they were playing. Following them was a crowd of jeering Egyptians, brandishing their fists in the air and shouting. Robert, James and Lucy could understand them.

'Freedom! Independence now!' The Baxters shrank back amongst the palm trees, sensing danger. Then, around thirty British soldiers in khaki uniforms with white helmets and carrying batons, entered the park and passed between the marching band and the protesters to form a cordon, preventing the angry mob from advancing any further. The mood turned uglier. Up to now the protesters had simply been noisy, but now they started to push and shove against the line of soldiers. The band left the park, but now more soldiers arrived, some on horseback, and the tactics changed. Pairs of baton-wielding soldiers dived into the crowd and grabbed individuals, carrying them writhing and struggling back to military trucks that had pulled up at the entrance to the park.

As the battle drew level with the Baxters, Lucy looked away, appalled by the violence she was witnessing, but turned back when she heard James shout:

'Look!' She followed the direction of James' finger, pointing into the crowd. Robert was quicker to react. With a standing start that his sports coach would have been proud of, Robert dashed into the melee and scooped up a small boy who was sitting, dazed, on the ground. It was a miracle that the crowd hadn't already trampled him underfoot. Robert returned to where James and Lucy were sheltering beneath a group of palm trees and watched as the crowd passed by them. By now, the Baxters had witnessed many Egyptians, some of them unconscious, being carried to the trucks. As the protesters started to disperse and the army lorries drove away, Robert, James and Lucy moved out into the open, hoping they could reunite the boy with his parents. The soldiers were gesturing and shouting at the stragglers in the park.

'Go on! Clear off! Scarper! Vamoose!' One of them turned towards the Baxters.

'Oi! You. Scram! Wot you waitin' for? Get outta here.'

'Excuse me!' said Lucy angrily, 'We're looking for this boy's parents.'

'Oh! You're English, are you?' replied the surprised

soldier, 'Well, you should skedaddle. It ain't safe here. Anyway, he's just a local. Whatsit matter to you?'

'Honestly! Some people!' muttered Lucy under her breath.

'Come on, Lucy,' said James. Let's walk through the park and leave by the other gate. Surely his parents will notice us; we're hardly inconspicuous!' It was true; the little boy in Robert's arms maintained a constant and very loud wailing.

'Do you know this boy?' James asked everyone they passed, but they all shook their heads.

'Now what?' said Robert, pausing at the park gates. Lucy surveyed the scene. There were very few people left in the park who weren't soldiers, and none of them had given any indication of being interested in the boy's welfare.

'Back to our hotel,' replied Lucy.

Twenty minutes later, they were the only occupants of a small lounge in the Winter Palace Hotel. A waiter set down a tray bearing four glasses and a jug of iced water. He was clearly puzzled by the presence of a small Egyptian boy. Tears streaked the boy's dusty face and his whole body shuddered with occasional sobs, but the wailing noise he had been making as they entered the hotel had now subsided. Lucy held the boy's hand and spoke gently to him in Egyptian.

'What's your name, little one?' She figured he was around five or six years old.

'Gamal,' he stuttered, between sobs.

'Where are your parents?'

' Beni Murr village.'

'I'll find out where it is,' said James, leaping up out of his chair and trotting to the reception desk. He returned a few minutes later, shaking his head.

'They've never heard of it.'

Lucy continued her questioning. 'Is Beni Murr village a long way from here?'

'Yes.'

'How far?'

'I don't know.'

Lucy tried another approach:

'How did you get to Luxor from Beni Murr village? '

'We came by train.'

'So, did it take a long time?'

'Yes, it took hours.'

'Hours?'

'All day. It's a long way to Alexandria.'

'Alexandria?' repeated Lucy in amazement.

'Where's that?' asked Robert, turning to Lucy.

'It's hundreds and hundreds of miles away. We are in the middle of Egypt, and Alexandria is right up at the top, by the sea.'

'And you live in Beni Murr village?' Lucy asked the boy.

'No.'

'But why did you say you did?'

'I didn't. You asked me where my mum and dad are.'

'Yes, that's right, so…'

'So that's where they are.'

'Allow me,' said James to his sister, springing to his feet, 'Your line of questioning isn't going awfully well.' He peered at the boy, his face screwed up into a funny expression, scratching his head and looking puzzled. The boy had stopped sobbing now. Then, James jumped up in the air and pointed at him.

'You, Gamal. There is Beni Murr village.' James pointed to the next table. He skipped over and sat on it.

'You came on a train. Chuff, chuff, chuff, whoo, whoo!' Gamal laughed. 'We are here. In Luxor,' cried James, leaping to his feet. 'Is this where you live?' Gamal nodded. 'See, Lucy, it's easy when you have a gift. And so, Gamal, my friend. Where in Luxor do you live?'

'I don't know.'

'Who do you live with?' asked James.

'Uncle Khali.'

'Ah!' said James, spinning around, making Gamal laugh again.'

'Now we're getting somewhere. Did Uncle Khali bring you to the park?'

'Yes,' replied Gamal, tears welling in his eyes. 'I lost him. We were listening to the music and then lots of men came and started shouting, and then soldiers came and they started fighting, and I lost him.'

'Can you remember anything about where you live?' asked Lucy.

'It's near my school. I haven't been there long.'

'I don't suppose you can remember the name of your school?'

'El-Nahassin Elementary School.'

Robert raced back to the reception desk, almost knocking over his Uncle Archie on the way. He briefly explained the situation, and shortly afterwards, they returned from the reception desk to join the others.

'Hello Gamal,' said Archie, 'I believe you have lost your uncle. I'm an uncle too, and I'm always getting lost, but these three always find me. I think your uncle was in the wrong place at the wrong time, but I'm sure we can find him. Tonight, you can stay here at the hotel with us, and in the morning we will take you to school. Then we will find out what has happened to your Uncle Khali.'

The following day, the four Baxters were lunching in the hotel restaurant and discussing the events of the day. It had started very smoothly. Archie was now the proud owner of a Crossley 25/30, a large, blue, boxy car with a flat roof that the army had once owned. They had all travelled to Gamal's school, where his teachers welcomed him warmly. They knew nothing about the previous day's events. The school promised to send someone to find more members of Gamal's family. Then Archie dropped Robert, James and Lucy back at the hotel. He visited the prison where the army was detaining the demonstrators and discovered that Gamal's uncle was there.

Now, Archie was recounting what had happened.

'It didn't look too rosy at first. The corporal on the desk wasn't at all interested and told me to 'Get lost'. I'm afraid I had to do something that I don't like doing; I had to namedrop.'

'I can see why giving my name would give you results,' chipped in James.

'Shut up, James!' came the familiar refrain from Robert and Lucy.

'I had no choice other than to mention that Lord Carnarvon is a friend of mine. You can imagine the scenario.'

'Sarge, there's this geezer says we ought to let one of our prisoners go.'

'Sorry to trouble you, Lieutenant, there's a fellow says we've arrested the wrong bloke.'

'I say, Major, spot of bother, chap says he knows Lord Carnarvon,' and so on, right up the ranks to Lord Alfred Milner, who's in charge out here. Then all the way back down again. So, Khali Hussein was reunited with his nephew in the end. I don't think anyone has thanked you for your bravery, Robert, rushing into the crowd to save Gamal.'

'Oh! That's okay; I didn't give it a second thought. It's just great to get a good result.'

CHAPTER FIVE

'I have some news for you,' said Archie, rubbing his hands with glee. 'We're going on a little trip. It turns out that Howard Carter and Lord Carnarvon will be delayed a few weeks whilst they sort out permissions with the Egyptian Government. You have to have a licence to dig in architectural sites in Egypt. Anyway, I have an open invitation for us all to visit a young lady further north. Her name is Mary Chubb and she has since been described as 'the first professional excavation administrator.' She works for the Egypt Exploration Society and this is their second year excavating in the ancient city of Amarna. I met her at an exhibition in London and I happen to know, because she told me, that she loves children.

'Cool!' replied Robert.

35

'Is it far?' asked Lucy, ever practical, 'Or is Big Bessie going to take us there?'

' I've got something much more fun lined up for you. We are going to hitch a lift.'

'What! Stand in the middle of the desert with our thumbs out?' asked James.

'No, no, no. I've managed to get us a ride on a Vickers Type 56 Victoria. It's a Royal Air Force transport plane, and it's brand new. They're erm, testing it.'

'So, there will be a test pilot, and we are the test passengers,' retorted Lucy, rolling her eyes in exasperation, 'We're in a foreign country, a long way from home, both in distance and in time. We've already experienced a riot. Don't you think we are in enough danger as it is without going looking for it?'

'I'm certain you will get on very well with Mary,' said Archie after an awkward silence.

The following morning, just after sunrise, the Baxters were all standing on the runway looking with mixed emotions at the aeroplane that would take them to Amarna. Archie had a smile as wide as his face. Loving all things mechanical, he knew what the plane would look like, but he had only seen one in a military museum before. He couldn't disguise his glee at the thought of flying in one. Lucy's mouth was wide open in horror.

'But, but, it's got four wings and propellers; it's a biplane. Look, there are only two engines to lift that massive brute!' she exclaimed.

'Well, all planes have propellers in 1922, the jet engine hasn't been invented yet.' explained Archie.

"It could be worse,' said James, goading his sister, 'It could be made of paper and balsa wood.'

'Actually, admitted Archie. 'I do believe that the frame

in these earlier models is constructed of wood, but it doesn't use paper.'

'That's it! I'm not flying in that!'

'But, but, we have to,' spluttered Archie, 'It's all arranged with Mary.'

'I didn't say I wasn't going to Amarna; I'm just not flying in that death trap! I trust Big Bessie; I don't trust that.'

'Big Bessie?' queried James.

'Look, am I right in thinking that if I stand behind the pillar where we arrived in Karnak at five o'clock, Big Bessie will take me back to the lab?'

'Yes, but we will be there in a couple of hours,' protested Archie.

'And,' continued Lucy, 'Therefore, I can set Big Bessie's coordinates to take me to Amarna, and I can get there at the same time as you.'

'Well, yes…' admitted Archie.

'You shouldn't go alone. I'll come with you,' said James, recognising that once his sister had made up her mind, there would be no stopping her. 'Robert, you go with Uncle Archie.'

'In the death trap,' added Lucy.

***

James and Lucy watched the transport plane slowly climb into the sky. Lucy was worried about Robert and her uncle's safety, but they hadn't appeared to be the slightest bit concerned. Then, she and James returned to the hotel to eat lunch before walking to the temple at Karnak. As they passed through reception, the manager rushed out to intercept them.

'I am glad I've caught you. A man came to the hotel this morning and left this for you. He told me that it's a gift

37

for the family who helped his nephew.' he said, handing James a small box. Lucy and James opened it and took out four brass medallions, each on a chain and inscribed with the words: "Gamal Abdel. Forever at your service."

'Cool!' said James, clutching the medallion to his chest. The manager looked on bemused as James continued to speak, 'This is such an honour. Proof that dreams can come true. I wish to thank my brother and sister. Without their help, winning this award would not have been possible. And back in the lab, a big, big thank you to Bessie, not to mention Uncle Archie who…'

'James! Stop that now!' commanded Lucy.

The manager returned to his desk, smiling at the antics of these strange foreigners. He wasn't to know that in seven years time the first Academy Awards, the "Oscars", would take place and that James regularly rehearsed his winner's speech for the day when he would win one.

***

James and Lucy spent the afternoon at the temple in Karnak. Whilst Lucy studied the art and architecture, James, with his new language skills provided by Big Bessie, spent his time chatting to tourists from all around the world, trying to convince them that he was a native countryman of theirs. Invariably, he failed, leaving them puzzled. Although his accent was very convincing, James generally knew next to nothing about the various countries they came from, so he found it hard to maintain a conversation. He especially enjoyed talking to a group of Italians because it allowed him to use a wide range of hand gestures when describing his favourite snack. They were horrified that anyone might consider putting pineapple on a pizza.

At five o'clock, James and Lucy waited behind the correct pillar - easy to identify amongst the hundreds of others because it was near a statue of the god Amun. Shortly afterwards, they felt the familiar sensation of Big Bessie whisking them back to Uncle Archie's lab.

'No!' said Lucy sternly when James had proposed ordering a pizza, 'Apart from the fact that Mrs Simpson might be around, you've already had breakfast and lunch. It will be lunchtime when we meet Robert and Uncle Archie in Egypt, so no doubt you will have another meal then. So, no. Oh, I do hope they have arrived safely.'

'Okay,' sighed James, 'Well then, the sooner we get off, the sooner we can be eating lunch. There aren't any new messages from Big Bessie and you've set the coordinates, so let's go.'

***

'How was it?' asked James.

'Tremendous!' replied Archie

'An experience,' added Robert. 'Noisy, bumpy and uncomfortable, but it was certainly an experience.'

'Unfortunately, because we came here by Big Bessie, we will have to go back to Luxor the same way,' explained James with mock sorrow. Lucy said nothing; she was just relieved that Robert and her Uncle had arrived in one piece.

'Let's go and find Mary Chubb,' said Archie.

Mary Chubb welcomed the Baxters warmly. She was in her mid-twenties, had long, dark hair tied back loosely in a ponytail and wore a pretty, floral, cotton dress.

'I'm so pleased that you could join us,' Mary gestured with her hands, describing the sweep of the cliffs arcing away from the Nile and returning to the water several miles away to the south. 'This, as I'm sure you know, is Amarna. Originally it was called Akhetaten, which means 'Horizon of the disc'; the disc being the sun god. We are standing outside our headquarters, 'The Dig House'. It was adapted from one of the original Egyptian buildings dating back three thousand years. Come inside; there is a shady courtyard, and Abu, our houseboy, will bring you some nice cold water.'

Young Abu was dressed in an ankle-length robe so white that they almost needed sunglasses to look at him. He gave them a broad smile as he set down the tray of glasses, before retreating inside the building.

'Judging by how clean his clothes are, I don't suppose young Abu does a lot of digging,' chuckled Archie.

'Oh no, perish the thought. I came out here with two chaps from England, Hilary and Ralph. Like me, it's their first time. John is the field director and is here with his wife, Hilda, and there is Tommy too; they were all on this site last season. Then there are about forty Guftis, men and women from a village called Guft a couple of hundred miles away, near Luxor. Generations of villagers from there have been carrying out excavation work. The Guftis mostly wear blue or black robes, and they supervise the local villagers who do all the heavy digging. Abu and his family are from a village to the north of here and see themselves as a cut above the rest.'

'How long have you been an archaeologist,' asked Lucy.

'Oh, I'm not an archaeologist. I'll tell you how I ended up out here in Egypt,' said Mary. 'I took on a secretarial job for the Egypt Exploration Society. All I wanted to do was earn a little money to continue with my sculpture course at The Central School, in London. It was a very dull job; I was bored. The Society only took me on because the secretary had too much work, but then she wouldn't give me anything interesting to do.'

'Control freak,' said James, nodding. Mary paused and

seemed to make a mental note of this interesting new expression.

'Well, one day, I was sent down to the basement to search through a packing case for a drawing. I had to delve right to the bottom. I found the drawing, but there was another object in the crate. I unwrapped something hard and found myself holding a broken piece of ceramic tile decorated with a flower. Sand slipped through my fingers, Sahara sand, and then something happened. It was as though a light had been switched on inside me. I was holding something that had been held by the archaeologist who had found it, then before that, perhaps the last person who had touched it was an Egyptian, thousands of years ago.'

'So what did you do next?' asked Robert.

'I came back to the office in a daze. Then I saw the chaotic, jumbled notes that the men excavating in Egypt had sent, expecting us to make sense of them and type them up, and I thought, "What the Society needs is a secretary out there in the field." So I suggested it to the Committee and they agreed, and…'

'And the rest is history,' finished James with a grin.

Refreshed by slices of watermelon that Abu had brought them, the Baxters stumbled outside into the bright sunshine, following Mary along a well-trodden path through the sand, that led to the excavation site. They noticed low walls, all that was left where once houses stood.

'We're excavating a house just like one of these,' said Mary. 'The walls looked just the same as these low ones, but actually, it's a two-storey house, completely covered in sand. To start with, the men can dig quickly, but as they get closer to the level of where the floor once was, they have to be more careful as that is where they might find objects of interest. It's then that the experienced Guftis take over. If the men find something worthwhile, we record it, and then when they receive their wages at the end of the week, they get an extra payment, depending on the value of the find. It's called baksheesh and helps motivate them to take extra care.'

Fifteen minutes later, a colourful pageant unfolded before them. A man using a tool shaped like a large, flat hoe scooped the sand into a rope basket, then a child would pick it up and join the long line of other children, chattering cheerfully as they walked towards the area where they dumped the sand. The boys were dressed like the men, in once-white ankle-length shirts, their heads wrapped in a turban or a small grey felt cap. The girls wore black shawls on their heads, but their cotton dresses were every colour under the sun.

'We are very excited,' said Mary, 'Because we have discovered a painted stone lintel that was once positioned over a doorway. From the inscriptions on it, we know the name of the man who lived here three thousand years ago. His name was Nenwef, and he was an administrator. Just fancy, I don't know who lived in my little room in London fifty years ago, yet yesterday I was cataloguing a necklace that probably belonged to Nenwef's wife, centuries ago.'

'Look over there!' cried Robert. From behind Nenwef's house came eight Guftis, carrying a large stone block resting on a latticework of bamboo poles. They walked steadily, singing in time with their marching feet.

'That's the lintel I was talking about,' explained Mary. They are taking it back to the Dig House. Everything found is photographed and measured, and then drawn. We have marked the whole area out on a map in squares to record exactly where we find objects. I happen to know that this house is T.34.1. A little more exact than saying 'opposite the third boundary stela'.'

'Stellar, like a star?' queried Lucy.

'No, s-t-e-l-a,' explained Mary. 'The Pharaohs would commission them to mark the boundaries of a city. See over there, carved into the side of the cliff. They are massive monuments to celebrate how great the king was. They have inscriptions or images on them and sometimes both. Originally, the Egyptians painted them in bright colours, but they have been eroded by the wind and the sand.' Lucy nodded. She realised that Big Bessie had set her down beside one of them at the entrance to the city. Now she knew what it was called.

'Oh good, here comes lunch. It's Abu and his Uncle Hussein,' announced Mary.

'I presume there will be sandwiches,' said James with a grin, 'Get it sand...wiches.'

'James,' said Lucy in the low, warning voice she used when James started to get silly. As it happened, there weren't any sandwiches. Hussein presented them with a box, inside which was a large cottage pie that he had kept warm by surrounding it with straw. It was delicious and was followed by fruit, chocolate and lemonade.

After lunch, the party split into two. Robert and James stayed with their uncle and explored more of the site. Mary had work to do, cataloguing the artefacts discovered that week, and Lucy was very keen to help her if she could. Mary showed Lucy how everything had to be labelled and cross-referenced with a scale drawing and John's photograph. Mary gave Lucy a bracelet to copy, thinking it would just be something to keep Lucy occupied but she was astounded by the quality of the drawing.

'Why, that's just as good as anything I can do, if not

better!' exclaimed Mary. 'I wish I had you here all week; I'm rather behind with the work.'

'Hmm! I'd love that,' replied Lucy. An idea was beginning to form in her mind.

All too soon, it was five-thirty, and the daylight was beginning to fade. Archie, Robert and James returned and described their day.

'It was good fun.' said Robert, 'One of the men let me use this short hoe thing. He called it a tourieh. Anyway, not only did I get a good workout - I don't want to lose my upper-body strength - but I gave the local guy a rest and a good laugh watching me. I also spent some time helping Hilary and Ralph survey the site. I had to hold up this long stripy stick whilst they looked through an instrument and wrote down measurements. As for James, well…'

'I was raising morale,' said James, 'I was watching a group of children carrying the sand away and they were singing a song which went like this: 'W'Allah negib! W'Allah negib!'

'By God! We're bringing it along!' translated Lucy.

'Exactly,' replied James, 'But it got a little monotonous after a while, so I taught them a new one. Do you remember that kookaburra song from being a kid? "Kookaburra sits on the old gum tree. Merry merry king of the bush is he," and so on. Well, I had them singing it as a 'round', and it was a hoot. Every time a pair of children passed me, they had to start the verse again and then keep going until they returned to the dig to get more sand.'

'Did you teach it to them in English?' asked Lucy.

'No need. Thanks to Big Bessie, I could teach them in Arabic. I can't say for certain they know what a kookaburra is, though.'

***

Lucy tugged at Archie's sleeve. The evening before had been very pleasant. They had enjoyed a meal cooked by Abu's uncle that was every bit as tasty as the food served in the hotel in Luxor. Archie, James and Robert slept in the Dig House lounge, whereas Lucy had a camp bed in Mary's room. It was almost time for them to leave and begin the journey back to Luxor.

'Can I have a word outside, Uncle?' Lucy whispered. Once she knew they couldn't be overheard, she continued, 'Uncle, I want to ask you something and I'm hoping you will say yes. Please can I stay here another week? I've had a brilliant time and I could carry on helping Mary with her work. I know I would learn such a lot, and it won't make any difference to you because I can set Big Bessie to arrive in Luxor just after you get there. I set Big Bessie to pick James and me up at six o'clock from the stela at the entrance to this city every day. James can go now. He's used Big Bessie on his own before and I laid out the runic blocks for him to use to get back to Luxor anyway. Then I can follow on in a week, so we will all get back at the same time. Mary said I could sleep in the spare bed in her room. Please say yes, Uncle.'

'You've thought it all out, haven't you,' replied Archie. 'Well, I'm impressed with the setup here, so I can't see you coming to any harm. You know how to operate Big Bessie as well as I do, so I think the answer is definitely a yes. Come on, let's tell the others.' James' reaction was quite typical. It allowed him to say something he often said:

'What can possibly go wrong?' He meant it as a joke, but the trouble was, invariably, something did go wrong.

CHAPTER SIX

If Robert had thought that the plane journey to Amarna had been uncomfortable, then the trip back to Luxor was ten times worse. It was a case of turbulence with a capital' T'. Every now and then, they would drop a few feet, big dipper style, then slowly climb back to their correct altitude. Robert and Archie were the only passengers. The co-pilot came through to speak to them.

'Sorry chaps, this crate can't take any more. She's handling a little tail heavy, and there's a wind picking up. We're not too far from Luxor, but it's going to be safer to put her down as soon as we can. There's a little airfield nearby. I'm sure you can make some alternative travel arrangements from there. Can't be helped.' Robert wasn't at all unhappy. He was feeling quite unwell and would be

47

relieved to be back on solid ground.

***

'Hmm!' said Archie dubiously, staring a camel with very bad breath full in the face. There was the small matter of an area of desert to cross. Archie pondered, the camel chewed.

'Come on, Uncle,' urged Robert, 'It will be a laugh. I've never ridden a camel before.'

'I think the camel master is having a laugh, considering how much he wants to charge to take us across the desert. Oh, okay then,' sighed Archie.

Three camels trudged across the desert sands, slowly climbing dunes and steadily descending the other side. Archie and Robert were following Ali, their guide. They had been riding for nearly an hour, and the novelty had worn off for Robert. It was very, very hot, but the wind was picking up. The trouble was it wasn't a cooling breeze; it was as though someone had turned on an extremely powerful fan heater. Robert had a large shawl wrapped around his head, which he was grateful for, because it protected his face from the stinging sand. The guide turned his head towards Archie and Robert and pointed upwards. They had set out under blue skies, but now there was a yellow ochre cloud reaching up from the horizon, and it was coming their way. Then, in a matter of seconds, it was upon them. The sky grew darker and darker until finally it was as dark as night, and the air was thick with swirling sand.

Robert's camel was not happy. None of the travellers was enthralled with the situation, but his camel was particularly disgruntled. Now that it could no longer see the others, it decided that the solution would be to outrun the storm, and it bolted. Robert found it exhilarating for a brief moment, then he realised it was actually quite scary. He wasn't in control, but not only that; his stomach felt decidedly queasy and his head hurt. He couldn't see where they were going but he sensed the camel was climbing a dune. Then, as though the camel realised that running was not such a good option after all, quite suddenly, at the top of a dune, it stopped and sat down to sit out the storm. Unfortunately, this took Robert by surprise, and when the camel dropped to its knees, Robert somersaulted over it's head and then rolled and slid down the dune. All went black.

'Robert!' Archie was shouting as loudly as he could, 'Robert!' Archie was puzzled. He was standing next to the camel that Robert had been riding. It was still sitting on the sand, chewing silently, oblivious to the alarm and panic building within Archie. The skies had cleared now, but there was still a strong wind blowing a layer of sand across the ground, obliterating footprints. He could see the shawl that Robert had been wearing lying halfway down the dune, but there was no sign of the boy. Surely he wouldn't have set off across the desert on foot?

'I look,' said Ali, the guide, still sitting astride his camel and pointing in the direction of the next dune. He set off and Archie made his way down to where Robert's shawl lay. As he picked it up he was startled to hear coughing and spluttering a little way further on. Then to his astonishment, the sand danced strangely in front of him, and he heard Robert speak. Now he knew what had happened.

'Uncle?' said Robert anxiously, 'Has what I think has happened actually happened?'

'I'm afraid so, my boy. Apart from a light dusting of sand, which is fading by the minute, you seem to be invisible. Are you hurt?'

'No, I feel a little groggy, but I think I'm okay to climb back in the saddle.'

'Hmm! Slight problem. We can't let the guide know you are invisible. I know! There's a blanket rolled up on the back of your saddle. Wrap that around you.'

'Okay, Uncle, but after a few minutes, the blanket will turn invisible.'

'Ah, yes, of course. In that case, I'll give you mine too, and you'll have to keep swapping. Ali, our guide, told me that we are almost at the edge of the desert. He will be riding at the front. I'll just have to try and position my camel so I'm in between you and him.'

Thirty minutes later, the party reached a road that led to a village not far from Luxor. Ali was worried about his eyesight because, occasionally, he had looked back to check that all was well and he could have sworn that the camel at the back was riderless. When he rubbed his eyes and looked again, he could see the figure of the boy, swathed in a blanket, astride the camel. Ali blamed the storm for getting sand in his eyes and upsetting his vision. Shortly after they had passed a house with a 'taxi' sign fixed to the wall, Ali heard a shout calling him back.

'I think we will get a taxi from here,' announced Archie, standing next to his camel, which was now sitting at the side of the road. Ali looked for the boy, who was nowhere to be seen. 'He's over there. Call of nature; he's not very well,' said Archie, gesturing to a wall beside the house. 'It's okay; you can go now.' Robert wasn't on the other side of the wall. He was standing very quietly and very invisibly beside his uncle.

As Ali headed back the way they had come, a generous tip stuffed into his pocket, he thought to himself:

'Crazy Westerners. If they had waited a while, they

could have got a bus from the airport that would have got them to Luxor just as quickly.'

***

James was waiting for them in the hotel. He was on the veranda, stretched out on a cane chair with his feet on a footstool, sipping a glass of iced water.

'You took your time, Uncle,' he said with a grin.

'Don't ask,' muttered Archie.

'Where's Robert?' asked James.

'I'm here as well,' replied Robert ruefully, 'My turn to be invisible.'

'Oh, hard luck,' replied James with genuine sympathy. 'We knew it was likely to happen to one of us. I've nothing to report from the lab. There are no new clues from Big Bessie about what we've come here to find.'

'Can you two amuse yourselves here today?' asked Archie as he slumped down in a chair next to James. 'Lucy will be along later. I suppose we should have decided on a time so we could have met her at the temple, but never mind, I'm sure she will just jump in a taxi. This afternoon I want to look at a truck that's for sale. I think it might be very useful. Lord Carnarvon doesn't know it yet, but Howard Carter's expedition will need one this year. They will be here later this evening. First of all, though, I'll just rest my eyes for a moment. It was a tiring journey.'

'What's that around your neck, James,' asked Robert. Before James had finished explaining about the medallions they had been given, Archie was already snoring.

'Brilliant,' said Robert, 'I'll wear mine now. I'll put Lucy's on too, and I can give it to her when I see her. It's funny she's not here yet. She's usually early for everything. Anyway, I think Archie's got the right idea. I'll tell you about our journey, and then I think I shall have a little snooze myself.'

***

At that same moment, Lucy was copying inscriptions carved into a fragment of stone.

'It's called a cartouche. They always take this form in Egyptian art,' said Mary, 'It's an oval, with a straight line either below or above it, and inside are hieroglyphics giving the royal name of the pharaoh. This part here translates as: "In his name as Shu, who is in the Aten." Shu was the powerful god of the air and was the sun's protector. He also helped determine whether you went to heaven after death or were eaten by a monster god called Ammit.'

'Yuk, gross!' replied Lucy.

'And the Aten, that was the sun god. All-important here in Amarna because the whole city was built to worship Aten. The pharaoh chose it because it was an area of empty desert. No one had lived here and worshipped other gods. Its original name was Akhetaten, which means Horizon of the Aten. As you have seen, it's very sunny here.'

'All this information is fascinating,' said Lucy. 'I hope I get to use it one day.'

***

Archie couldn't help worrying about Lucy. He knew she could confidently zoom backwards and forwards in time, but he was surprised that she hadn't arrived back in Luxor. Everything else was in place. He had sorted out the transport arrangements for Lord Carnarvon and Howard Carter's expedition. He had dined with them the previous evening and had requested a meal to be taken up to James and Robert. The servant had looked a little surprised by the quantity of food he was taking to be consumed by just one boy; he couldn't see, of course, that Robert was also in the room, licking his lips in anticipation. But where was Lucy?

52

Archie decided to telephone her.

'Hello, Lucy,'

'Uncle! How nice to hear from you. I'm with Sue and Ralph in the office.'

'Ah! I appreciate that your side of the conversation might be overheard. I was partly ringing to see how you are.'

'Oh, it's going fine, Uncle. I'm learning such a lot about Ancient Egypt.'

'Good, good. I'm also a little concerned because you haven't arrived here yet. I wondered if there was a problem.'

'Not as far as I know, Uncle. But, I'll make a note of today's time and date so that I won't programme Big Bessie to bring me back to Luxor before now. You wouldn't be ringing me if I was already there.'

'Yes, quite.'

'How long to the … the discovery?'

'Oh, we have four days yet.'

'That's alright then; I look forward to being there. How was your journey back? I was worried about you.'

'Oh, erm…it took a little longer than expected,' replied Archie dismissively, conscious that Lucy's fears had proved to be correct, 'But we're all back safe and sound.' He thought it best to remain silent about Robert's condition until he saw Lucy face to face. There was no point giving her something else to worry about. 'We all look forward to seeing you. Bye for now.'

'Bye, Uncle.'

***

Back in twenty-first-century Cambridge, there were slim pickings in Archie Baxter's kitchen for the little grey mouse. He checked all the usual places, but no one had been here since he last visited. He didn't realise it because he had never lived anywhere else, but living in an old Georgian house made for a comfortable life. He could usually find enough food to eat, and travelling around the house was easy. He squeezed under a tiny gap in the skirting board and slipped down to the space beneath the floor. It wasn't food he wanted now; he was thirsty and knew just where to go.

The mouse scampered along between the joists. He changed direction by wriggling through a notch cut into timber for a wire to fit through and arrived at the site of his current project. Several days before, he had been chewing a plastic pipe that ran between the floorboards for no other reason than curiosity. It didn't taste particularly appetising, but what had surprised him was that, when he chewed further, a thin jet of water sprayed out. At first, he had scampered away in fear, but when he plucked up enough courage to return, he discovered that the water fountain he had created was altogether a good thing. It was even easier to drink there the following day because a small lake had formed.

Now, as he surveyed the scene, he saw that it had changed again. The water fountain still sprayed a thin jet of water in a gentle arc, but the lake had gone, and the surface he walked on had changed. If he had been a builder, he would have known that the ceiling had been constructed by nailing thin strips of wood, or laths, to the joists, which were then plastered over. Now, although the laths remained, the sodden plaster had fallen into the room below. However, he was just a mouse and didn't need the world explained in such detail. He peered through the hole in the ceiling and watched the water drip, drip, drip onto a huge, frightening contraption looming beneath. He didn't like the strange noises it was making, and he wrinkled his nose at an acrid smoky smell. He had a quick drink from the water fountain and then retreated to a more familiar part of the house.

CHAPTER SEVEN

Robert, James and Archie had crossed the River Nile on a small ferry and now, after a short donkey ride, they were gazing at the cliffs soaring either side of them. It was their first sight of the Valley of the Kings. They sat on a rock and watched the scene. It all looked rather confusing as the local workers gathered in groups to await instruction. Nearby they could see Archie talking to two men. One was in his late forties. He sported a bushy black moustache, a bow tie, a dark linen jacket, a white shirt and a Panama hat. They presumed he was Howard Carter, the archaeologist. He seemed impatient and kept looking at his watch. The other man looked around ten years older and was of slighter build. He wore a tailored, three-piece tweed suit that looked more expensive than his companion's and leaned on a walking stick. He had to be Lord Carnarvon, the man Archie referred to as Herbie. He and Archie shared jokes several times, but Howard didn't join in. No one took any notice of James, and, of course, they couldn't see Robert. Finally, the three men shook hands and walked off in different directions, with Archie returning to where Robert and James were sitting.

'All is going well,' said Archie. 'They were pleased with the arrangements that I had made, although Herbie laughed at me for buying such a big truck. He admired my optimism. If only he knew what I knew. He'll need it to transport all the treasure to Cairo! He's flying to Spain today to watch the Villafranca Grand Prix.'

'Did they ask why you are here just with me, instead of three of us?' asked James.

'No, they didn't ask, so I didn't give them any explanation. Howard is very focused on the job at hand. He hasn't time for small talk.'

'I know,' said James with a grin, 'He's got tunnel vision, get it? He spends his time tunnelling into the ground and…'

'Shut up, James!' said Robert and then felt regret that his sister wasn't there to join in. 'What did Lucy say when you telephoned her this morning, Uncle?'

'She was surprised that I was so concerned and said she was enjoying her time there. Actually, I think she will get more out of her time in Amarna than she would here in the Valley. She's with a friendly little team who are giving her individual attention. That's not possible here because it's a bigger setup. Herbie's funding it and he's a wealthy man; he married into money. I worked out the value of the marriage settlement he received from Rothschild, the

American banker. In today's money, it's equivalent to fifty-nine million pounds.'

'Wow!' exclaimed James, 'I'm willing to give up my bachelor status for that amount of money.'

'It won't work like that,' laughed Robert. 'That's about how much you will have to pay to persuade someone to marry you!' Sensing where Robert was sitting, James gave him a playful push. If anyone had been watching them, they would have noticed the sound of laughter and a strange indentation in the sand made by an invisible boy tumbling off a rock.

***

For the next two days, Archie and the boys felt they were in limbo. Lucy still hadn't arrived. Archie telephoned every day, and learned that she was working hard, happy to be part of the team. He couldn't understand why Lucy hadn't finished her week in Amarna and then returned to the lab to reset Big Bessie to come to Luxor a week earlier. She should be with them by now! There wasn't much for them to do in The Valley of the Kings. Archie had made all the transport arrangements but Howard Carter largely ignored them, as he had his own assistant.

It was the 4th of November and Archie knew it was an important day. He made sure that they were in the Valley early in the morning.

'I think we are close to the right spot,' said Archie to Robert and James. 'It's hard to say. Ah! There…look… that boy, carrying a canister of water. I think it's him we are waiting for.' The boy trudged along, bearing his heavy load on the way to provide water for the men digging nearby. Then, suddenly, he stumbled, tripping over a large rock.

'Ow,' He set the canister down to rub his toe and then froze for a moment. He dropped to his knees and scrabbled away at the sand around and under the rock. He had discovered a hole and he pushed his arm into it, then quickly withdrew it, perhaps just in case a snake was sleeping under the rock. Then, abandoning the canister of water, he ran off in the direction of the digging men.

Soon, a dozen men encircled the rock and worked together to lever it aside. Luckily there were no snakes. Even luckier, after brushing away the sand, they discovered a step. Archie knew that this was the first of a flight of stone steps that would lead to the entrance of Tutankhamun's tomb. The men started singing and shouting and slapping each other on the back. There was a lot of excitement in the air and, eventually, one of the diggers brought Howard Carter to the scene.

'That's about it for us today,' said Archie. 'They have around four days of digging to do before they get to the bottom of those steps. We may as well head back to the hotel and have a meal that doesn't taste of sand. Then, after that, I think we should head up to Karnak and, with Big Bessie's help, we'll go and look for Lucy. It should be her last day in Amarna today so we could meet her halfway - in the twenty-first-century.'

They noticed the water carrier, who was also watching the scene. He looked astonished when James approached him and said, in fluent Arabic:

'You must make sure you get decent baksheesh for this. You deserve a big bonus. Don't let the other men claim all the credit. You've just made history!'

***

It was nearing the end of the working day. Mary and Lucy had been called away from the office to help with the dig. There was another exciting discovery in the house where they had found the lintel. The Guftis had dug up a large clay jar buried below the original floor level and it was full of silver coins and ingots.

'This could have been the house of a thief,' explained Ralph to Lucy. 'I wonder what happened to him to prevent him from returning for his stolen booty? We'll take this back to the Dig House immediately. It might prove too much of a temptation for a poor local farmer if we leave it here. We'll come back and dig up this whole area. There could be more buried treasure.'

'It's a godsend,' said Mary, turning to Lucy. 'Our society is so short of funds that we're unsure if we can afford to come back next year. At the end of the season, we take everything to the museum in Cairo. They keep a lot of it for themselves, and so they should, but they let us take some of it back to England. Much of the silver isn't of great historical value, especially the ingots, which the thief probably melted down from jewellery, so this find may help fund next year's dig.'

***

Later that day, Lucy was packed up and ready to leave.

'Are you sure you don't want me to accompany you to the ferry?' asked Mary.

'Oh no! I'll be fine.' Lucy knew that Mary thought she was travelling by train back to Luxor. 'I know the way, and I'm used to travelling all over the place by myself. You've got far too much work to do cataloguing all that silver.'

Lucy set off alone. The real reason she didn't want any company to the ferry was because she wasn't going that far. All she had to do was wait out of sight beside the large inscribed boundary stela at the entrance to the city and, twenty minutes later, Big Bessie would do the rest.

Coincidentally, at that very moment, Archie, Robert and James were in the Karnak temple. They were waiting

61

for Big Bessie too. Archie was looking forward to seeing Lucy.

'Just think,' said Robert, just before Big Bessie whisked them all away, 'In a few minutes, we'll be able to telephone for a pizza.' But he was about to be disappointed.

'That was a most unusual journey,' said Archie, the moment he arrived back in his lab, 'It was almost as though there was turbulence.' Then, not hearing a response from the boys, he looked to his right, then to his left. He couldn't see anyone.

'James, are you invisible too?' Still no response. Then it dawned on him; he was alone. Nothing like this had ever happened before. Archie leapt to his feet and rushed out from behind the glass screen to check Big Bessie's monitor, hoping that it might show where Robert, James and Lucy were.

'Whoah!' Archie's feet slid out from beneath him and he landed on the floor. He sat up with difficulty, paused for a moment, then realised that his bottom was wet. He was sitting in a pool of water! Gingerly, he got to his feet and peered under Big Bessie. The puddle extended underneath the time machine; thank goodness she was on legs and not sitting in the water. Then he noticed water dripping from Big Bessie. That was puzzling; Big Bessie was all-electric; water did not feature in her construction. Archie took a few steps back and scanned every part of the time machine. Nothing seemed amiss. Then he looked up and gasped in horror as he saw the large brown stain on the ceiling, at the centre of which was a small hole through which fell a steady drip, drip, drip of water. Archie rushed from the lab in search of the stopcock. He needed to turn off the water supply and find a plumber, fast!

CHAPTER EIGHT

'Whoah!' cried James. It was the same sound that Archie was making in the lab, but James wasn't slipping on a wet floor; he would soon discover that the Baxter children had slipped through time and space. After an extremely bumpy ride, James had landed face down on a paved stone floor. It took him a few moments to recover his wits, but before he could get to his feet, he heard a familiar voice.

'James!' It was Lucy. 'I got here a few seconds before you. I don't understand what's just happened. I thought I was on my way to meet you in Luxor. Where are Uncle Archie and Robert?'

'I don't know about Uncle Archie,' came Robert's

voice from a few feet away, 'But I'm here.'

'Where?'

'Ah! We didn't tell you because we didn't want to spoil your week in Amarna, but it's me who's turned invisible this time. James, did you know that you are wearing a pretty white skirt?'

'So I see. Very fetching. I think Big Bessie has gone off her rocker,' said James. 'She could have had the decency to make you visible again, Robert. Why has she sent us here?'

'Haven't a clue,' replied Robert. 'When is this?'

'I think we've gone way, way back in time,' replied Lucy thoughtfully. 'Judging by the hieroglyphics painted on the walls, we are still in Egypt, but look at them. Look at those painted pillars; the colours are so bright, they look new!'

'What shall we do?' asked Robert.

'We should wait here, I think,' replied Lucy, 'We're not in a tomb, it's too spacious, so I guess we are in a temple. I think we must have travelled back over two thousand years. Someone is bound to come along eventually.'

'You're still wearing your medallion, James,' said Robert, 'I've got Lucy's around my neck. Shall I take yours, James, then it will go invisible too?'

'Good idea,' said James, taking the medallion off and showing it to Lucy, 'It was a present for saving that boy in Luxor. You've got one too.'

Maya walked, deep in thought, towards the inner sanctuary. He was the High Priest of the temple of Amun in Karnak; you couldn't get any higher than that! Citizens from the two lands, Upper and Lower Egypt, flocked to this temple bringing offerings of food, beer, oil and perfume to please the mighty god Amun, the god of the air.

In distant quarries, sculptors were carving statues to celebrate Amun. His storerooms were overflowing with golden treasures. The wealth of his temple rivalled that of the Pharaoh; his temple owned more land than the Pharaoh. Maya was powerful, and he should have been contented. He ought to be spending his time worshipping the gods, especially his beloved Amun, but instead, he was worrying, because change was in the air. No one in Egypt liked change, except for, it seemed, the Pharaoh, Amenhotep IV. Maya had learned that the Pharaoh had ordered extensive building work in the east of Karnak. That in itself wasn't unusual. It was the fifth year of Amenhotep's reign. All new kings liked to order statues and temples to celebrate the gods, and perhaps more importantly, to show what a great and powerful ruler they were, but Maya was hearing strange and worrying rumours about this young Pharaoh.

Suddenly Maya stopped. He could hear voices. How could that be? This part of the temple was his private domain. It was too early for the next religious ceremony. Surely no one could have wandered in from the public areas of the temple; doorkeepers would have stopped them. He crept forward to hide behind a column and observe. He hadn't climbed so high in the priesthood by being impetuous, so he wasn't going to go charging in to confront the intruders until he had assessed the situation. To his amazement, he could see two children looking at the wall paintings, but what was even more bewildering was that, although he didn't understand the language they were speaking, he was sure that he could hear three voices despite there being only two of them.

'I'll tell you what's really strange,' said Lucy. 'Can you read everything that's painted on these walls?'

'No,' replied James. 'I can read some of the writing,

but not those pictures you are looking at. I thought they were just decoration.'

'Same here,' added Robert.

'Some of them are just pictures, describing scenes from the past,' explained Lucy, 'But there are also hieroglyphics. I can read them all! I learned a tiny bit about them in Amarna, but it's as though Big Bessie has boosted by ability. I can't wait to tell Uncle Archie.'

'I wonder where he is?' asked Robert.

'Maybe Big Bessie has taken him home,' suggested James, 'I hope so, or else how can we ever get back?'

Maya decided that the children posed little danger to him. He figured that only two people had the authority to have brought the visitors to this part of the temple and not worry about angering the god. One was the Pharaoh himself, Amenhotep IV, and the other was his Queen, Nefertiti. That seemed more likely because the Vizier, Nakht, the Pharaoh's senior advisor, had told him that Nefertiti was to visit him that morning.

Maya strode into the centre of the chamber. The Baxters turned to face him, bowed their heads and waited for him to speak, unsure of the etiquette. Maya was reluctant to admit that he didn't know why the children were there. He was used to a more obsequious greeting from strangers; they should have fallen to their knees at the very least. Maybe they were a foreign prince and princess?

'What are your names?' he asked. Whilst he had heard them speaking another language, Egyptian was the language of the most powerful and important country in the world, so he presumed they would understand him. He was proved right because the girl answered with a clear and educated accent.

'I'm pleased to meet you. My name is Lucy.' Then the

boy spoke:

'My name is James.' Robert kept silent.

'I saw that you were studying the walls,' stated Maya.

'Oh yes,' replied Lucy, 'I especially like this story about how Amun was the Creator God and was the first to stand on dry land.'

'Curious,' thought Maya, nodding sagely, So she could read hieroglyphics! Only ten per cent of the population could read. Mostly they could only read hieratic, a shorthand version of writing; very few people could decipher the hieroglyphics that Lucy appeared to be reading with ease. James also nodded, but it was to cover up the fact that he wasn't as skilled at understanding Egyptian symbols as his sister. However, he had no problem with speaking the language.

'Please forgive us, we don't mean to take up your valuable time, but we know that we have been brought here for a purpose, so we wondered how we might serve.' He considered adding, 'Your wish is my command,' but he felt it might be a little cheesy.

'Time?' echoed Maya, 'Time! Why it's almost time for the ceremony, for "Drawing the Bolt." Stay where you are and wait.' Maya wasn't sure if he should let these two children witness the ritual, but he sensed their motives were pure, and if anyone could judge a person's character, he felt that, as High Priest, he could. He turned towards an enormous door at the end of the room and clapped his hands three times. It was only then that the Baxters noticed two men guarding the door. They swung it open and allowed dozens of other priests to enter the chamber. They followed Maya to a door on the opposite side of the temple, and doorkeepers pulled it open. Lucy gasped; she could see that inside this shrine was a statue, and it was one she had seen before. It was of the god Amun, and now she knew they were at the temple in Karnak. In her own time, this city would be called Luxor, but she knew that in this time it was called Thebes. The statue had white fabric draped around it. Some priests removed this 'clothing' and took it away, whilst others dressed the statue with fresh material. The Baxters could see that food and water had been placed at the foot of the statue. That, too, was removed by priests and replaced with fresh offerings. Throughout this activity, Maya was chanting:

'I come to you, oh my God, oh boy of the gods, the eternal of the two lands. Oh sanctified hand, oh Amun, master of the two feathers, protect the king of Upper and Lower Egypt.'

A young priest entered the room, walking so fast that he was almost running. He waited a moment, standing close to Maya, who stopped chanting, and he whispered something. Maya acted swiftly. He clapped his hands three times and all those attending the statue retreated from the shrine. Priests closed the shrine doors, and everyone left this part of the temple until only Maya, the doorkeepers and the Baxters remained. Maya stood motionless in the centre of the room, his head bowed. Lucy and James copied his stance; perhaps this was a period of silent reflection? It wasn't; Maya was waiting for someone. After a few minutes, the door was opened again. Whilst there had been some females amongst the priests who had participated in the ceremony, none had the presence of the lady who now walked into the room. Her clothes were adorned with gold; she wore a tall white hat, topped with two ostrich feathers and her hair fell in ringlets to her shoulders. A necklace comprising five rows of gold, turquoise and red beads encircled her long neck. In short, she was breathtaking.

Lucy gasped in amazement and then noticed the reaction of the doorkeepers. They dropped to their knees and then prostrated themselves before the woman. Lucy dug James in the ribs and hissed:

'Copy me.' James did as he was told.

'Don't think that I don't know which god is in that shrine,' the woman announced.

'My Lady of Grace, welcome,' said Maya, 'Life, Prosperity, and Health. How can I serve you today?'

'We must appoint a new High Priest to serve the sun god, Aten, as Meryamun will shortly be passing on to the afterlife.'

'Yes, of course, Lady of the Two Lands, but I am afraid that I feel my place is right here in…'

'I wasn't asking you,' she replied sharply, 'The High Priest will be Ibebi. I have come to collect the scrolls so the scribes can update the "Book of the Dead" with new spells before Meryamun's funeral. '

'Yes, my Queen of Great of Praises,' replied Maya meekly, although inwardly seething. There was a period of silence in which he felt he was under scrutiny. Then to deflect the focus away from himself, he pointed to James and Lucy, still stretched out on the floor. Now that they were down there, they had no idea when they were supposed to get up.

'I have been very impressed by the reading abilities of this girl, Lucy, whom I presume has been sent to serve you.' The Queen looked down.

'Rise!' she said in a commanding voice. Lucy and James scrambled to their feet.

'I don't want any more boys,' she said, glancing at James, 'Even if his hair is the colour of the setting sun. But the girl…' she clasped Lucy's chin between her fingers and turned her head from side to side, 'Interesting bone structure. And the hair, is it yours?' She pulled Lucy's hair.

'Ow!'

'You read? Show me. What does this say?' Lucy began to read the hieroglyphics on the wall. 'Stop! Do you write and paint?'

'Yes, Queen of Great of Praises,' replied Lucy, remembering how the High Priest had addressed her.

'Then you will do.'

'Please, can I ask not to be parted from my brother,' pleaded Lucy.

'Don't be impertinent, I have decided.'

'Do you not know your place?' demanded Maya. 'You dare to ask the Lady of the Two Lands, Queen Nefertiti, to change her mind!'

'I'm sorry,' mumbled Lucy, bowing her head.

'Hmmm!' murmured Nefertiti, as she turned away, 'I might sell this red-headed one into slavery.' She paused as she heard Lucy gasp, 'Then again, I don't think I will because he reminds me of the sun, so I think he should stay here under the care of Maya as a constant reminder of the one true god. Now, Maya, I want to see the scrolls I asked for. Show me.' Nefertiti and Maya retreated to an alcove, giving Robert, James, and Lucy a chance to confer.

'I don't think we have a lot of choices, but where should I go? With you, Lucy or with James?' whispered Robert. Lucy thought for a moment.

'I think you should stay with James, Robert. Two reasons; firstly, I will probably be easier to find if I'm with the Queen, whereas we don't know where you will end up, James. Secondly, I might be in some kind of all-female area where you might feel a little uncomfortable.'

'Are you sure?' asked James anxiously, 'I can't quite make Nefertiti out; she is very expressive with her hand gestures, and the way she speaks is a little strange. It's almost like she's acting.'

'Yes, I'm sure it will be for the best. I don't feel particularly brave, but I have faith that Big Bessie will help rescue us at some point. Oh, shush! They are coming back.' Robert squeezed Lucy's arm. Nefertiti walked past the Baxters and headed in the direction of the door.

'Come!' she announced, turning towards Lucy, who promptly fell in behind her after kissing James on the cheek. Nefertiti paused and addressed Maya:

'I insist that you find this boy something useful to do. I have people who will keep me informed. Make something of him.' Maya clapped his hands three times. The doorkeepers opened the door and Nefertiti, followed by Lucy, left the room as Robert and James looked on helplessly. When would they see their sister again?

CHAPTER NINE

Nefertiti and Lucy walked away from the temple and headed towards the Royal Palace. Several servants and bodyguards had fallen into line behind them.

'That's quite enough exercise for one day,' said the Queen, and she stopped and clapped her hands. Dozens of servants came running, carrying a large covered chair mounted on two long poles, and set it down beside her.

'Come along, Lucy; there's room for two,' said Nefertiti. They sat side by side, and the servants hoisted the poles onto their shoulders. 'Tell me in all honesty, what do you make of the High Priest of Amun?' Lucy felt a pang of terror. The Queen had commanded her to be honest, but what if she said the wrong thing? There didn't seem to be any love lost between Maya and his Queen, so she took a deep breath and spoke:

'He did seem rather pleased with his position in life. '

'Go on. Be more direct. Three words, all starting with the same letter.'

'Boastful bragging bully.'

'Again.'

'Smug, snooty, snob.'

'Again.'

'Pompous priestly prig.'

'Haha! I think I'm going to like you.' laughed Nefertiti. 'You're not Egyptian, so where are you from?'

'I'm from England. It's a long way north of here. It's very cold and wet a lot of the time.'

'Ughh!' Nefertiti shuddered, 'Why ever would anyone want to live anywhere where the sun god, Aten, can't reach them. It makes no sense? Anyway, I like your honesty, and I feel that coming from outside, you might have a refreshing way of looking at the world. I tell you, things are going to change around here.' Lucy nodded, but her face betrayed that she was worried about what was going to happen to her brothers. Lucy would come to discover that, despite the Queen portraying herself in public as vain and preoccupied with her own beauty, (after all, 'Nefertiti' meant "the beautiful one has come"), underneath all that she was very, very clever. She guessed what was troubling Lucy.

'Don't you worry about that red-headed brother of yours; he will be safe. He has a cheeky face and a twinkle in his eye. I'm rather hoping he will be a thorn in the side of High Priest Maya.' Lucy felt a little reassured. 'Oh dear!' said the Queen feigning sorrow, 'I quite forgot to tell Maya about the opening of the new temple. He's going to be taken by surprise. What a pity.' The doorkeeper who let his

Queen and the young blonde stranger pass into the palace wondered what they were finding so funny.

***

'I suppose I ought to decide what I'm going to do with you,' said Nefertiti. 'How old are you?'

'I'm twelve.'

'That's the age that many Egyptian girls marry; they often have had a baby before they are thirteen.'

'Oh no! I'm not ready for that.'

'Very sensible. I was fifteen when I married the Pharaoh, my Ami.'

'Gosh! Are you going to have any children?'

'Going to? I've already got three.'

'Have you? I'd love to meet them. If they've inherited your looks, I bet they are really pretty!' Lucy thought about how the conversation might develop if they were in her own time. By now, Nefertiti would have been showing Lucy photographs on her phone. 'Are there any paintings of them on the walls of the temples?' asked Lucy.

'No.'

'Oh, that's a shame. I've seen many paintings and sculptures of men, but not many of women and children, apart from a few dancing girls. I think the family should feature more. '

'I think you are absolutely right,' replied Nefertiti, 'I know I feature quite a lot, and so I should as the King's favoured wife, but I'll have a word with Seti, Amenhotep's advisor. Things are going to change around here and that's a very small change, compared with what's to come, but it's a change nonetheless.'

***

'You are looking quite magnificent today, your Majesty,' purred Seti, 'Let me adjust your headdress; it will

75

be perfect if I just tip it back a fraction. Such a regal shade of blue.' Seti wasn't a popular man, but the Pharaoh Amenhotep IV liked him, which was precisely why the upper echelons of the court despised him. Seti knew how to smooth out the King's insecurities, boost his ruler's pride and steer him down a particular path so that the Pharaoh thought all his decisions were of his own making. Now the Pharaoh's chest puffed up with pride. He clearly thought he looked magnificent too!

'It's important for me to inspire a feeling of awe in my people,' said Amenhotep. 'After all, it is me that the sun god, Aten, speaks to, so my appearance must be spectacular, it must be striking and glorious, and then the people will bask in my radiance.'

'Indeed, you look splendid, your Majesty. Will you be wearing that headdress at the ceremony or your blue and gold one?

'Oh, the blue and gold, it will catch the sun's rays beautifully. Everyone will be dazzled.'

'That won't be the only thing they remember when we, I mean…when you open the new temple in Karnak. I hope I can see Maya's face when you announce all the changes,' chuckled Seti.

'I wonder what Nakht will make of it?' pondered the Pharaoh, 'He is a very efficient Vizier. I do rely on him to administer the kingdom, so I don't want to upset him.'

'I'll have a quiet word with him. He's likely to have a lot more gold to play with in the future. He won't turn his nose up at that.'

'Oh! You mustn't think that money is my prime motive for change.'

'No one could doubt your devotion to the god, your Majesty. Of course, with more money we…I mean, you, can build more statues of yourself to emphasise your good relationship with the god, Aten. The key message is that to have any kind of relationship with Aten, your subjects must achieve that through you. The god speaks to you and you only.

***

Maya looked across at James with annoyance. As if, as High Priest, he wasn't busy enough already, satisfying the needs of the god Amun, without having to take responsibility for this red-headed foreigner! What to do with him? The Queen had made it clear that she expected James to do something useful. Before he could make a decision Maya needed to discuss something with Asim, one of his senior priests, but he didn't want to leave the boy alone in the temple's inner sanctum, so he would just have to follow along.

Thirty minutes later, James was left sitting outside the doorway of a room in a different part of the temple complex. He was quite content, he had found a shady place to sit, and he amused himself watching dozens of young priests at work. There was a high stone table close by, an altar for the god Amun, and the priests were laying down offerings of food and beer beside it, ready for a higher-ranking official to set it out. James wasn't concerned about the discussion inside the room because his invisible brother had slipped inside to eavesdrop.

'May the god Amun be forever in your house,' said Asim.

'And may he show generosity to you and all those who work with you,' responded Maya. 'What news have you for me? What of the Pharaoh?'

'The situation is confusing. As you know, we sent our representatives to buy stone from several quarries. They have been unable to do so because of a mandate from the King. Yet I saw barges laden with stone heading upriver. Why would that be? It can't be anything to do with the new palace the Pharaoh has commissioned here.'

'Have you seen the new palace?' asked Maya. 'It's to celebrate Aten, isn't it? I haven't felt inclined to visit it,' he added dismissively.

'I tried, but I was barred from entering. The guards told me it wasn't safe. They seemed to be letting others through, though. Anyway, you will have your opportunity. I presume you've been given your invitation?'

'What invitation?'

'To the opening of the new palace. The Pharaoh is making a proclamation. We are all expected to go.'

'This day gets worse and worse,' moaned Maya. To top it all, the Queen has landed me the job of finding some meaningful work for some red-headed foreigner!'

Robert's ears pricked up. What was going to happen to James?

'Might I make a suggestion?' said Asim, 'How about helping at Per Nefer. What more noble calling?'

'Excellent!' replied Maya, smiling for the first time in several hours.

***

In the East of Karnak was a district called Per Aten. It was there that you got the best view of the setting sun. Right now, it was midday, and Maya surveyed the scene before him. Many of the notable citizens of Thebes and surrounding districts were gathered in the courtyard of the new temple, Gem Pa Aten, waiting for the Pharaoh to arrive. Enormous statues of the King flanked the area and what made Maya even more disgruntled was that everyone was forced to stand outside, under their gaze, beneath the blazing sun. This temple didn't have a roof. It was taking the worship of the Sun God, Aten, too far!

It took a little ingenuity for James and Robert to get into the temple as they weren't on the guest list. Three guards stood outside the entrance, and Robert simply poked each one in the back and continued until they were all arguing with each other. Then he and James slipped inside. They moved to the back of the courtyard and looked up at the sculpture of Amenhotep, standing atop a pillar towering twenty feet above them. The impression given was that there was nowhere you could stand in the temple without being watched by the Pharaoh.

'It's all me, me, me!' whispered James in English, so no one would understand what he was saying.

'Too right. The great I Am,' agreed Robert. That view was reinforced when the Pharaoh arrived, his chair positioned on a platform carried by at least fifty servants. Behind, in a smaller chair, came Nefertiti, and in a group of women walking behind them, Robert and James were relieved to spot Lucy.

Eventually, Amenhotep began to speak:

'Long live the good god, the lord of heaven, lord of the earth, the great living Aten who illuminates the two banks, the beloved of Aten, the King of Upper and Lower Egypt...'

'He does go on a bit, doesn't he?' whispered Robert. 'I'm going to sneak through the crowd and try and speak to Lucy. If she can get away, I'll suggest we meet up outside the walls of this temple.'

An hour later, Lucy managed to slip away and meet up with her brothers. The speech was over and the Pharaoh and the Queen were involved in a series of religious rituals.

'Well, I'm stunned!' said Lucy.

'To be honest,' replied Robert, 'I kept drifting off. He didn't half repeat himself a lot. What was that all about?'

'Change,' replied Lucy. 'Nefi said there would be some changes, but I didn't expect them to be so big.'

'Nefi?' queried James.

'The Queen, Nefertiti.'

'So what's changing.'

'Well, first of all, he's changing his name - instead of Amenhotep, he's going to be called Akhenaten. That means "beneficial to Aten" So, at the moment, Nefi calls him Ami, but she's going to have to start calling him Aki.'

'Aki sounds a bit wacky to me,' quipped James.

'Shush,' warned Lucy. 'Someone might hear you. Anyway, then basically he said that the gods have ceased their appearances, one after another, and now there was only one god who was effective, the Sun God, and that he was the only one who could talk to him.'

'I told you he was on a power trip,' said Robert.

'But there's more,' said Lucy urgently. 'The big news is that we are moving.'

'Who's moving?' asked James.

'The whole of the court is moving. He's ordered a new capital city to be created, and I am leaving next week with the Queen.'

'But where is it? How can you create a new city, just like that.'

'To answer your last question first, he can because this is the richest and most powerful country in the world. Apart from riches, it's got plenty of manpower. And secondly, I'll tell you where it is. I recognise the name of the city; it's called Akhetaten. It means 'Horizon of the Aten'. Its modern name is Amarna; it's a long way north, and we've been there before when we stayed with Mary

Chubb.'

***

Not for the first time, Archie listened to a sharp intake of breath as Billy surveyed the scene. He had rolled up the rug in the lounge and taken up a floorboard that ran almost the entire length of the room.

'Now, there's your problem, see,' he said to Archie, who was standing beside him. 'It's what comes wiv using plastic pipes. I doesn't hold wiv 'em myself. You can't beat usin' copper. Nuffin' better. There, see them? Them's mice droppings, them is. If I was you, I'd 'ave all this out and replace it wiv copper. I mean, I could cut the pipe, whack a straight connector on it and be finished in half an hour, but what's to stop them chewin' through the pipe somewhere else? Let me tell you about this job I was called to...' Archie listened to the plumber's tales of disaster for five minutes before interrupting.

'Okay, so if you were to do as you suggest, when would you be able to do it, and how much will it cost me?' Archie had already turned off the water supply to his apartment and placed several industrial-sized dehumidifiers around his lab to suck the water out of the damp room. He had taped a piece of card over the hole in the ceiling to prevent a curious tradesman from peering down and asking questions about the odd-looking machine below. Now he just wanted Billy to go. He had more important things to worry about than the cost of the repairs, like three lost relatives, for instance, not to mention trying to fix Big Bessie once she had dried out.

'Well, there's a lot of work to do. I'm not sure when I can fit it in, but I'm sure I could move a few jobs around. It won't come cheap, mind. The cost of copper has gone up again. Who did this work anyway? Let me tell you about......'

CHAPTER TEN

James tried unsuccessfully to engage the priest in a chat and eventually gave up, following him on the long, hot walk to start his first day of employment in Thebes. He had to resort to a secretive game of tig with his brother. Needless to say, Robert, with his competitive spirit and the advantage of being invisible, was the victor. Eventually, they arrived at a large, square tent close to the Nile, well away from other buildings. Three sides of the tent were open.

'You should have told me we were going camping,' quipped James, 'I haven't brought my sleeping bag. "Ging Gang Goolie...everyone join in!' The priest ignored him and had a few words with a guard at the entrance, then he turned on his heel and walked away.

'Not inclined to help me settle in, then,' said James quietly to Robert as they approached the guard.

'Wait,' said the guard before entering the tent and conversing with another man. The guard returned to his duties, and the second man walked over to James.

'I am Hapu. We had very little notice that you were coming. It doesn't matter because you can start at the beginning of the process by bringing in the natron.' He pointed to a well-worn path leading back towards the river, 'You will find a pile of sacks on the landing stage by the river.'

'Natron? What's that? It sounds dangerous!' Hapu looked at James in disbelief and then realised that he had to make allowances. Despite the boy's use of the language, he was, after all, an unsophisticated foreigner.

'Natron. It's a salt. We use it for washing, cooking, and of course, considering where we are, as a preservative. Stack it behind the tent.'

Both boys were pleased to discover that they weren't overseen for much of this task. Robert was pleased because he felt he was getting out of condition, having had no exercise other than a little light jogging. Here was an opportunity to work on his upper body strength. James was pleased for obvious reasons. All he had to do was carry the heavy sacks of natron when he was within sight of the tent, after which Robert could take over. It still took a few hours, but that was evidently quicker than Hapu had envisaged because he looked surprised when James appeared back at the entrance of the tent.

'Woah!' yelled James, which luckily drowned out the gasp from Robert. Neither of the boys had ever seen a dead body before, but there was a very naked and very dead man stretched out on a stone slab. It was a large tent, and they were aware of others working inside but they were transfixed by the sight before them.

'Come. You are lucky,' said Hapu, 'We have just received the body of Meryamun. Well, we call him Mery. He was a high priest. May Osiris look kindly on his soul. You can witness the beginning of the process.' Then, seeing James' reluctance to step forward, he said again, 'Come, come.' Robert's hand was resting on James' shoulder, and very slowly, the twins shuffled towards the corpse then stood, aghast, at one end of the slab.

'He doesn't look very merry now,' thought James to himself.

'We've already purified the body - I washed him in water from The Nile and palm wine,' said Hapu cheerfully, 'Next on the list, we have to clear out his head. It's full of useless stuff that will rot if we leave it there.' Hapu was holding a long metal spike. 'Pass me that hammer.' James did as he was asked and then was horrified to see Hapu poke the spike up the dead man's nostril and hit it hard with the hammer. 'It would make my life a lot easier if skulls were empty instead of being full of this blobby stuff.' Hapu turned, hoping to get a reaction from James. 'What? Where are you?' He walked to the foot of the stone slab. James had reacted alright; he lay flat on his back in a dead faint. 'By the gods!' Hapu picked up a handy jug of water and poured some onto James' face. James spluttered back to life, and Hapu turned to reach for another tool. James had blocked Robert's view of Hapu's handiwork with the spike and hammer, so he was unaffected by the gruesome turn of events, and was able to help his brother get back to his feet.

'I'm sorry,' said James, 'It's probably because it's been a long time since we...I mean, I, ate anything.'

'We'll stop soon. We'll just get this bit finished, and I reckon we'll call it a day. So, next, we use this little beauty,' said Hapu, holding up a metal rod with a hooked end. 'They don't call me Hooky Hapu for nothing. I can clear out this head in an instant; I just stick it up the nose, like this, and wiggle it about until it's all mashed up, then afterwards we just turn him over, and it'll all drain out of the nose into a bowl. Then we can throw it away. Do you want a go? ….What in Osiris's name…?' Once again, James was flat on the floor and this time, unseen by Hapu, so was Robert!

***

James and Robert walked to the tent with great trepidation to begin their second day assisting High Priest Meri to enter the afterlife. They had prepared themselves for what they might see when they arrived. Meri was now lying face down on the slab, and below him was a bowl which contained watery gunk, resembling a pink milkshake - the brains that had dribbled out of his nose.

'Hello boy,' greeted Hapu cheerfully. 'How was your room. Did you get something to eat?'

'Yes, thank you.' James and Robert had slept in a small outbuilding and had eaten fruit and bread that was so coarse it had the texture of sand. James had wondered if you could make bread out of the desert.

'You can give me a hand to turn him over,' said Hapu, 'You grab his feet.' James steeled himself, and they flipped the dead man over. 'Right, I'll show you what we do next.' Hapu picked up a very sharp-looking knife. Robert came up close behind James and held him tightly around the chest. They had discussed it earlier and had a plan. Robert was to close his eyes and be there to support James should he faint again. 'So, we've emptied his head of all that gooey stuff.

He won't be needing that in the afterlife, but he will need the stuff in here.'

Robert felt the full weight of James' body as once again he lost consciousness for a moment. What Robert couldn't see, with his eyes tightly closed, was that Hapu had inserted the knife into the side of Meri's stomach and cut an opening.

'Are you alright?' asked Hapu, 'How do you manage to stand in that funny position?' Luckily, James was just coming to and heard the question.

'Oh, it's a gift,' he said as he straightened himself up.

'Here we go,' Hapu pulled out what seemed an endless stream of intestines, and then with a deft flick of his knife, they lay coiled up in a large clay bowl. 'Put that out of the way,' he said. 'Mind you, keep them in view. We don't want any wild dogs running off with them. Our friend Meri here is going to need them in the afterlife. Meanwhile, I'll get on with getting the rest out - his stomach, his liver and his lungs.'

After a while, Robert and James were transfixed by the sight of the four bowls of Meri's innards lying sloppy, bloody and inert.

'I'll tell you what happens next. I'm going to have a beer. I reckon I deserve it. Nice neat job that. You, my friend, are going to wash this little lot. Take them out, one at a time, and give them a soak. You'll find some buckets of water from the Nile outside the tent. Swish them around with your hands. Then put each one in a clean bowl, bring them back and cover them with natron. The salts will dry them out. Make sure you tip that dirty water out well away from here. It's smelly enough in here as it is, which is why this 'House of Purification' is actually a tent with open sides.'

A few minutes later, Robert and James were crouched down, out of sight of the tent, trying to pluck up enough courage to begin their task.

'You've just got to look at it as a load of meat,' suggested Robert, 'Like a butcher preparing a batch of sausages.'

'When was the last time you prepared a batch of sausages?' asked James.

'Well, never, but you get the general idea. You've got to distance yourself from it.'

'I'd rather distance myself by running off,' replied James.

'We can't; Lucy might never find us. I'll tell you what. Close your eyes, stick your hands in this first bowl, and swirl it about. I'll tell you when to stop. Then we'll swap. I'll do the next one.'

'You'll have to get a bit quicker, my boy,' said Hapu. By now, James and Robert had washed all Meri's organs in Nile water and then in palm wine. They had covered them with natron and put them out of the way. 'Now, have you noticed that there is one very important part of our revered High Priest Meryamun missing?' James looked perplexed; Hapu continued. 'I'm surprised you haven't asked me already. It's the heart, of course, the most essential of all.' Robert thought to himself that perhaps all of the organs were pretty essential. 'Because, of course, that's the centre for all his intelligence.'

James wasn't the most diligent student in his school biology lessons, but he knew that Hapu was wrong. It was the brain that did all the thinking, that stuff that Hapu had unceremoniously pulled out of the dead man's skull.

'He will definitely be needing his heart if he wants admittance to the afterlife. Now there are some that take the heart out, wash it, and then put it back. But I don't hold with it. Where's the skill in that? I prefer to keep it in place, and then, when he gets to meet Osiris, the Lord of the Underworld in the Hall of Two Truths, he knows where it is,' said Hapu, 'Help me wash him in palm wine, and then we'll put him in a tub of natron.'

To start with, all went well. James felt he was getting used to handling dead bodies. Hapu and James began wiping Meri down with the wine. The problem came when Hapu asked James to wipe inside the body cavity. Robert noticed Hapu look over his shoulder and wink. Robert followed the direction of Hapu's gaze and noticed that everyone else in the tent had stopped attending to other dead bodies and were watching James and Hapu. Unfortunately, because of the proximity of Hapu, Robert couldn't get close to James. First, holding a linen cloth soaked in wine, James put his hand in the opening in of Meri's side. Then a cheer rang out from all the others in the tent. There was James, flat on his back on the sandy floor in a faint, once again.

***

James felt better now. A break, out in the fresh air, had done the trick, and he and Robert returned to the tent.

'Whoah!' cried James as he came face to face with a monster. Then he heard chuckling, and he realised that it was a man wearing the mask of a beast that completely covered his head. In fact, the beast was a jackal, and the man was Hapu.

'Feeling a little refreshed, are you?' asked Hapu. 'Our friend Meri is soaking in natron. We won't be seeing him again for seventy days, but as it happens, it's been seventy days since our next visitor had his salty bath, so, as we say in Per Nefer, the House of Vitality, life goes on.'

'But why are you dressed like that?' asked James.

'Because I'm the most senior priest here.'

'You're a priest?' blurted out James in amazement.

'Course I am. I'm a sem-priest; it's an important spiritual business this, preparing our people for their final journey. There are spells to read out once we start wrapping our next…client. So, that disqualifies you from getting involved in a hands-on kind of way. You can just hold things and pass me the stuff.'

'Well!' thought James, 'Compared with the rector at school, he's a very different kind of clergyman!'

'Come and meet Sadiki. He was a very important governor. It's not everyone who can afford all this care and attention, you know. Poorer folks get a very basic package, but for Sadiki here, there's no expense spared.' James and Robert could see the effects of the natron. Compared with Meri, Sadiki looked like a shrunken, wizened old man. His skin was blackened and leathery, and two attendants, maybe they were priests too, had set to work anointing the body with oils and perfumes. James' job was to pass linen bags filled with sawdust to them, which they proceeded to stuff into the body cavity to help improve the corpse's shape.

'Pass me those spices,' said Hapu, his voice muffled by the jackal's head he was wearing, 'The frankincense and the myrrh.'

'Frankincense and myrrh! I always wondered what they were for, you know, like in the bible stories, the gifts the Three Kings brought, although if I were to get a gift from a king, I would rather have…' At this point, Lucy or Robert would usually chime in with, "Shut up, James!" but all Robert could do was kick James on the shin.

'Ow!' Then it dawned on James what Robert was concerned about, 'Oh! Silly me, the bible story hasn't happened yet. Ignore me. Babbling!' Hapu shook the jackal's head in exasperation and continued to anoint the body with perfumes and oils. James stifled a laugh when Hapu placed two onions in the eye sockets.

'Onions! That's got to make him cry!' he thought.

Then the other men started to wrap linen bandages around the dead man, while Hapu, in the guise of the Jackal-headed god, Anubis, read spells to ward off evil spirits.

'You will live again forever. Behold, you are young again forever,' recited Hapu.

When the body was completely wrapped, James felt better about his role as fetcher, carrier and general dogsbody. Hapu asked him to bring over a bowl of gum, and this was painted over the bandages to make them stick together. Then the wrapping process began again. This time James had to stand holding a tray of amulets - lucky charms - some of which were placed between each layer of bandages. Sadiki's arms were crossed over his chest, and Hapu placed a scroll between his hands. Finally, Sadiki's body was covered in so many layers of bandage that it was now a coffin shape. Hapu placed a painted mask of Sadiki over his head, and the ritual was complete.

'Now for his organs,' said Hapu. He pointed to four bowls heaped with natron and then to four large jars. Each jar had a decorative lid shaped like a head. One was in the shape of a man; the others resembled animals.

'Do you know where the organs go?' asked Hapu. James shook his head. 'Then I'll tell you, one by one. Get the first one.' James gingerly delved beneath the natron and brought out a dried up, blackened bag. He held it up.

'Who would have predicted that I would be playing "guess the body part",' he thought.

'The stomach goes in the Duamutef jar,' said Hapu. Then, seeing that James still looked puzzled, he added, 'The Jackal.' James placed Sadiki's stomach in the jar that resembled a dog with pointed ears and added more natron. He put the lungs in the pot with the baboon's head, the liver in the one with a human head and the intestines had pride of place inside the container with a falcon's head.

'All done!' said Hapu, 'Time for a beer. He'll be collected tomorrow and taken in a sledge pulled by cattle to his tomb.'

'Jobs a good'un,' replied James with a smile.

'Now, no offence, but I don't reckon you are cut out for this line of work,' said Hapu kindly.

'No offence taken,' replied James. He completely agreed.

'You can come with us tomorrow to the tomb, there's usually quite a party, after all the sadness, but then I will be sending word to the High Priest Maya that he needs to find another outlet for your talents, whatever they are.' James nodded and gave him a double 'thumbs-up' sign. Hapu looked doubly confused at this action, thinking, 'This boy is odd!'

CHAPTER ELEVEN

First came professional mourners who smeared dirt on their faces and wailed loudly, pulling at their hair and clothes. Following them was Hapu, leading the funeral procession. They had all crossed the Nile in two large barges. A boat mounted on a sled and pulled by cattle was at the centre of the procession. It contained the coffin of Governor Sadiki who was making the journey to his tomb. Two young women knelt next to the coffin, portraying the goddesses who would guide the dead man to the afterlife. Priests burned incense and sprinkled milk on the ground as the family followed behind the sled, and last of all came servants carrying items that would be placed in the tomb for Sadiki to use in the afterlife. Finally, the coffin was stood upright in front of Sadiki's tomb, and Hapu moved a little way off to view the scene.

James and Robert joined him.

'Our friend, the lately deceased Sadiki, was from a very noble family,' commented Hapu. 'That's why he has the privilege of having a tomb here in this valley. Normally these cliffs, West of the Nile, are reserved for royalty, but his family have produced many girls who entered the Pharaoh's harum over the years. A more senior priest than me will do the next part of the ceremony; it's called 'The Opening of the Mouth'. Without this, the deceased wouldn't be able to breathe, eat or talk in the afterlife. There is a pause now because we are waiting for royalty. The Queen is coming. Oh look, there she is.' Another procession approached. At the head walked several guards, behind whom, carried in a chair, came Queen Nefertiti. 'That's what her name means, you know, 'The Beautiful One has Arrived', and how right that is.' James' heart skipped a beat as he scoured the rest of the Queen's entourage, and there she was, his sister, Lucy! Robert, too, had seen her and whispered in James' ear:

'I'll go.'

Once the servants had placed Nefertiti's chair on the ground, the ceremony commenced. A priest wearing leopard-skin robes stood in an apparent trance. When other priests 'awoke' him, he called out:

'I have seen my father in all his forms.' The other priests responded by calling on him to take the place of the God, Horus, to protect the deceased. Then, touching the face of the mummy with his finger and various tools, the priest recited some spells. When the ceremony had finished, Robert made his way over to Lucy. He whispered in her ear:

'Hi Lucy, this is all kind of weird, isn't it?'

'Robert!' she exclaimed, 'I didn't expect to see you

here.'

'Not that you can see me,' laughed Robert. 'If you look to your right, you might just see James in the distance.' Lucy searched for him, spotted him, and waved. James gave a discreet wave back.

'How are you both?' Lucy asked Robert.

'Oh, we've had an interesting couple of days. How about you?'

'It's been lovely. Nefi and I get along fine. Obviously, I was worried about you two, but she said you wouldn't come to any harm. We are sailing to the new capital tomorrow.'

'We have to go back and see the High Priest Maya next. It doesn't look like he's been invited here today.'

'No,' agreed Lucy, 'He and the Queen don't get on. Outside the tomb is a mortuary temple hall, and the relatives will be having a feast and party. We're going there. After that, I said I would show Nefi how to tie her hair, or rather her wig, in a French plait. '

'Bye, Lucy. Take care.'

'And you.'

***

The High Priest Maya scrutinised the red-headed nuisance standing before him. What should he do with him? Maya would much rather he didn't even have to look at him. Then he had an idea.

'I have an errand for you. I have a great fondness for the "Temple of Ramses, beloved by Amun". I want you to deliver an offering of incense there.'

'Sure,' replied James, 'No probs. Is it here in Thebes? I'll walk there now.'

'Walk?' said Maya, smiling at James' ignorance, 'If you were to walk, you might get there in about four days. It's in

Nubia to the South. I would travel on the Nile if I were you.' Then, as if talking to an infant, (which for James, as regards some aspects of ancient Egyptian life, was quite appropriate), Maya explained, 'If you haven't noticed, the current on the river flows south, but the wind blows to the north, so you need to find a boat with many oarsmen to row you there, and then you will sail back with the wind behind you.'

'Cool!' replied James. 'I've always fancied a Nile Cruise. Mixing with the top set.'

It turned out that James wasn't mixing with the upper echelons of Egyptian society. He and Robert were rowed to Nubia on a barge along with a hundred geese. Maya smiled when he heard, from the priest who had arranged the ride, reports of James' honking travelling companions. However, James wasn't too bothered about his noisy fellow passengers. It meant he could stretch out at the front of the barge and chat to Robert without being overheard. He felt guilty, though, that the boat was being propelled down the river through the efforts of dozens of slaves. Robert, always looking for sporty things to do, would gladly have helped row the barge.

By day three, the novelty of being on a river cruise had definitely lost its gloss. James and Robert were bored.

'I spy with my little eye, something beginning with 'R'', said James.

'River. I spy with my little eye, something beginning with 'M R.''

'More river. I spy with my little eye, something beginning with 'E M R.''

'Even more river. I spy…' Their game was interrupted by shouting from the rowers, who were pointing excitedly to the riverbank. To their horror, Robert and James saw a crocodile dragging a screaming young girl down a rocky path towards the river. Fortunately, the crocodile didn't have the girl's body between its teeth. It had clamped its jaws firmly around the girl's cotton dress.

'Come on, James!' shouted Robert pulling at James' arm, 'Let's go!' With all the commotion, no one noticed the gentle splash as Robert entered the water with a racing dive, but they certainly noticed the bigger splash as James jumped in.

'What am I doing?' thought James to himself as he followed his brother.

Naturally, being the stronger swimmer, Robert reached the riverbank first. All eyes were on James, though, not that Robert was the slightest bit concerned about being detected; he had set his sights on trying to save the girl. Robert saw some large rocks by the side of the path and ran over to them. As he reached them, two things happened; James struggled ashore, and the girl's dress ripped. For the moment, she was free, but she remained motionless, frozen by fear. The crocodile roared and opened its jaws wide.

'Quick!' yelled Robert, 'Grab the girl.' James did not need asking a second time; he raced to the child, grabbed her and then hauled her up the path, aiming to put as much distance between themselves and the crocodile as possible. He was just in time because the crocodile's jaws snapped angrily at thin air. If the croc was angry then, that was nothing compared to what he must have felt a moment later when a large rock smashed down on his head. The crocodile spun around in a fury; he could smell Robert, but he couldn't see him. He opened his mouth wide, baring rows of sharp, scary teeth, and roared. He then looked astonished as a rock shot from the side of the path, where the smell of human was strongest, and lodged itself between his deadly teeth. The crocodile reared up and shook his head, flinging the rock high into the air. Robert glanced up at the path and could see that his brother and the girl were now high up the trail. They were safe, so there was no point hanging around with the croc; they would never be friends! Robert climbed the path to join his brother. A group of men and women surrounded James, chattering excitedly. The girl had been scooped up by a woman, presumably her mother, and the men were slapping James on the back, taking turns to ruffle his hair.

'Where are you going?' one asked. Robert and James could understand him, but the accent was quite different from that spoken by the citizens of Thebes. James explained his mission.

'Why, that's just an hour's walk away. Come, it will be dark soon; you must spend the night with us and experience a Nubian banquet.' James beamed with delight. The diet on the boat of bread, bread and more bread was getting very tedious.

'Wait a moment,' James replied, 'I must get the gift, and, checking the path was free from crocodiles, he ran down to the water's edge to be met by a huge cheer. The barge had waited and the slaves raised their oars in the air and jumped up and down. No one was willing to get into the water in case the crocodile was lurking in the reeds at the side of the river, so one of the men threw the package of incense to James, who caught it and then gave a bow worthy of the Shakespearean stage before waving and returning to the Nubians.

***

'What a night!' exclaimed James as he and Robert walked along the bank of the Nile. Their Nubian hosts had rowed them across the river and then returned to work in the fields. Despite being poor, the Nubians had pooled resources to put on a feast to celebrate the rescuing of the girl from the jaws of the crocodile.

'Who knew there were so many things to eat in ancient Egypt that weren't bread?' mused Robert. 'All that fruit: raisins, dates, figs, melons, grapes, apples, watermelon. My taste buds were bursting.'

'I even enjoyed all that salad: the onions, lettuce and the cucumbers,' said James.

'Have you noticed, although they have plenty of flat bread, they don't seem to have tomatoes here, and the cheese seems to be more like a kind of cottage cheese? You know what that means, don't you.' asked Robert.

'I get your drift,' replied James, and they chorused together.

'No pizzas!'

'No burgers either,' said Robert. 'It's only the rich who can afford meat.'

'Also, there aren't any chickens either, just geese and ducks, so we can't even get any chicken nuggets!'

'After a talk with my coach at school, I promised myself that I was going to improve my diet, but it's not that easy getting a balanced diet if all you've got on the menu is bread. He also complained about my fluid intake. He said I should drink more water and not have fizzy drinks. It never seems to rain here, so I can't drink rainwater. There's plenty of water in the Nile, but that's not safe to drink. All everyone seems to drink around here is beer. I wonder what he would think of that!' The boys continued walking

'Oh, look! That must be the temple, James,' said Robert. Four huge seated figures were carved into the side of a cliff and in the centre was a doorway. The twins approached the first figure.

'I reckon that must be the Pharaoh. He's wearing that false beard that the Egyptian Kings always seem to like. I think he's got a big ego because all four of those statues are of himself,' said James.

'Yeah! And look at his wife and kids - they aren't even as high as his knees.'

'You can see who wears the pants in that house,' replied James

'Pants? It looks like he's wearing a skirt just like the rest of us!' They noticed a second temple a little further away.

'I'll take that back,' said Robert. There's another temple; it's smaller, but look, he's made the Queen the same size as him on the outside of that one. So this big one is more like a kind of man cave!'

A priest met James at the door of Pharaoh's temple and led him inside. Robert followed at a distance. Inside, the temple was lavishly decorated, with sculptures and paintings on the walls. Robert studied the images and noticed the many scenes of war, such as the Pharaoh riding in a chariot, shooting arrows, and lines of captured slaves. It was quite different from the chapel at his school! The priest led James into a second, pillared hall, and at the far end of the room were sculptures of four seated figures.

'Ramses II sitting alongside the gods,' explained the priest respectfully. 'It's a pity you were not here a week ago. The sun was at just the right angle to shine through the door and illuminate the face of Ramses. It only happens twice a year. Perhaps you can come next year.'

Robert and James thought about this conversation as they walked back to the Nile to return to Thebes.

'Next year!' voiced James. It's all very exciting here, but will we still be stuck in ancient Egypt next year? Come on, Uncle Archie, where are you?'

CHAPTER TWELVE

With his heart in his mouth, Archie prepared himself to press the start button that he hoped would send him back in time and heading in the direction of Egypt. Somewhere out there were Robert, James and Lucy, and it was up to him, with Big Bessie's help, to go and find them. He was worried because the water leak had damaged several of Big Bessie's circuit boards and wiped off important coding sections. He had spent hours and hours rewriting the code. Now that everything had dried out, he was fairly confident that Big Bessie would send him to Egypt, but would it be the correct year and the right district? He pressed the button and then quickly walked to sit behind the glass screen to await the moment of truth.

'Hmm!' he muttered to himself a few minutes later,

looking down at the clothes he was wearing. He had been expecting to see the baggy linen suit and polished leather shoes he had been wearing in 1922. Instead, he had on sturdy, black leather boots and a more practical khaki canvas jacket and trousers. He knew he was in Egypt. The four enormous figures carved into the side of the cliff told him so, but the boots he was wearing - what did they remind him of? Then he remembered. They were very much like the boots he had worn in his early days in the army. A shot rang out and Archie heard someone shout in Arabic. Slowly Archie raised his hands in surrender and turned to face the soldiers approaching him.

'Where do you come from?' yelled the Egyptian soldier sporting the three stripes of a sergeant. Archie decided it might be more advantageous not to let on that Big Bessie had given him command of the Egyptian language and remained silent, shrugging his shoulders in incomprehension. The Sergeant beckoned over one of the other soldiers.

'Woher kommst du?...d'où viens-tu?' Although Archie understood the question in both German and French, he waited until the soldier spoke in English. 'Where are you from?'

'Ah! I'm from England, from Cambridge actually,' replied Archie.

'Good university,' replied the soldier in English. Archie sensed that he could make a friend of this young man, but he didn't get the chance, as the Sergeant ordered the soldier to step back. The Sergeant seemed to understand that Archie was from England and, judging by the expression on his face, he was not best pleased about it. He gave several sharp orders to his men and, Archie was immediately shoved towards an army truck parked at the foot of the carved figures.

As he was bundled into the vehicle, Archie spoke to the soldier who understood English:

'What do you call this place.'

'The Ramses Temple? We call it Abu Simbel,' replied the soldier before being told to 'shut up' by his superior. The truck kicked into life and, creating a cloud of dust; it roared off to the army headquarters.

***

Archie sat gloomily in his cell, wondering why, once again, he was in this predicament. It had happened before, only this time he couldn't rely on the children to rescue him. It was the kind of jail familiar to those who, like himself, were fond of westerns; one side was sectioned off with bars from floor to ceiling, which meant the soldier on guard duty could keep an eye on his prisoner. By the same token, Archie could keep an eye on him too, and he had one factor in his favour: the soldiers did not know he could understand Arabic.

A door opened and two soldiers entered. One was the Sergeant. Archie had taken a dislike to him; he was gruff, bad-tempered and a bully. The other was the soldier who had acted as translator. Archie liked him. In different circumstances... Archie's train of thought was disturbed by hearing the exchange between the Sergeant and the guard who had been watching him.

'You are relieved of your duties. Report back to the guardroom.' The man looked relieved as he left the room; guarding the prisoner had been incredibly dull. Archie noticed the rifles that the soldiers were carrying.

'Surely those are Kalashnikovs,' he thought. 'Russian rifles. Not sure it helps me figure out what's happening. I don't even know what year it is.' The Sergeant barked out more orders to the young soldier:

'You are on guard duty now. Talk to him. See what you can find out. Any information would bring us credit. I'm going out to drink coffee. I'll come back in an hour to see what you have learned.'

'Any information would bring you credit, you mean,' said the young soldier quietly once his senior officer had left the room.

'Hello,' said Archie in English, 'I'm Archie Baxter.'

'Hello,' replied the soldier, dragging the chair the guard had been sitting on closer to the bars. 'I'm Ali.'

'I'm honoured to meet you, Sir,' replied Archie. 'You sound an educated man.'

'Not that it does me any good in this army,' retorted Ali bitterly. 'I went to university in Paris.'

'A beautiful city. When were you there?' asked Archie, hoping to gain some idea of what year it was now.

'I graduated three years ago.' That didn't help Archie discover the current date. 'I studied world politics. Now, as well as my service in the army and supporting my family, I'm trying to write a book about the political history of twentieth-century Egypt. At the moment, I'm researching the early life of our president.'

'You have children then; how many do you have?'

'I have three; two boys and a girl. They are very young. My daughter is still a baby.' Archie felt a pang of remorse thinking about the three children in his life and their current predicament. As he pictured the children, Archie's hand went unconsciously to the medallion around his neck, the companion to those that Robert, James and Lucy had been given. In the pause that ensued, Ali noticed what Archie was doing.

'What is that?'

'It was a gift from someone I helped rescue in Luxor back in 1922,' said Archie, taking the medallion off to show Ali. The young soldier studied it and read out the inscription:

'Gamal Abdel. Forever at your service.' Ali looked pensive for a moment, but then the peace was shattered when the Sergeant strode into the room. Ali sprang to his feet and saluted.

'Well?' demanded the Sergeant, 'Has he said anything?' Flustered, because he hadn't been interrogating Archie, Ali showed his Sergeant the medallion. The Sergeant glanced at it for a moment, then dashed it from Ali's hand. It clattered onto the floor.

'Suez! Has he mentioned Suez?' shouted the Sergeant. Ali shook his head. The Sergeant snorted, turned on his heel and left the room.

Meanwhile, Archie was experiencing a sensation as though a wave had washed right over him. Now he knew what was happening in Egypt right now. Although he didn't know the exact date, he knew that he was in the eye of a huge and dangerous International storm. The Suez Canal was one of the most important stretches of waterway in the world because it linked the Mediterranean Sea and the Red Sea; it meant that ships didn't have to sail right around Africa to get from East to West. He also knew that Britain and France had originally operated the canal, but that Egypt had nationalised it, which had prompted the English, French and Israelis to invade. Eventually, the Egyptians would be victorious, after a diplomatic stand-off between the Americans and the Soviet Union. Archie realised that he would have to choose his words carefully. He didn't want to reveal too much knowledge and get shot as a spy.

Ali picked up the medallion, and to Archie's surprise, rather than talking about the Suez Crisis, as it came to be known, he asked Archie to tell him in more detail about what had happened in Luxor back in 1922. Archie realised that here was another problem. It had all happened over thirty years previously. He didn't look old enough to have been an adult in 1922. So, when he recounted the adventure, he described his role as though he were Robert.

'And the boy. Where was his home village?' asked Ali. Archie racked his brains. It had only happened a few weeks previously, but all was blank until he had a mental picture of an actor from an old British soap opera wearing a woolly hat.

'Benny,' he blurted out, 'Benny something.'

'Was it Beni Murr?'

'Yes, I think so.'

'And the school. Can you remember its name?' Archie could; because he had driven there, he had had to study a map for some time to work out the route.

'El-Nahassin.' Ali paced up and down for a moment, deep in thought. He paused, then walked over to the guard's desk, where there was a telephone. Ali dialled a number and spoke softly into the receiver, the medallion on the table before him. Archie was surprised to discover that Ali was recounting his tale about rescuing the boy.

Finally, Ali ended the call and returned to sit next to Archie. After a few half-hearted questions about Suez, the conversation turned to more general topics concerning world politics; subjects closer to Ali's heart. Archie, of course, could draw on his knowledge of what would happen in the future.

'You see, the thing is,' said Archie, 'You may be used to the idea of Britain and France being at the top of the tree, especially as Egypt was a British Protectorate, but what I can see happening is that their influence will decline. It will be America and Russia that you will have to keep your eye on and then later, China.'

'China?' said Ali, laughing, 'They make cheap plastic toys!'

'Ah! That's just it. They make things and they have a big workforce. You will be surprised at how their economy will grow.' Just then, the telephone rang. Ali sprang to answer it. He listened, then did a strange thing; he stood to attention and called over to Archie:

'In Luxor, do you remember the name of the Uncle?'

'Yes, I think so. It was Karl, no Khali.' Ali repeated this into the telephone. Then once again he hung up the receiver and continued his conversation with Archie. They mostly talked about Paris, about experiences they had shared, like visiting the Eiffel Tower and the Louvre, when suddenly the door was flung open by the Sergeant. He was obviously angry.

'I don't know what meddling you've been doing, but I've been ordered to return him back to where we found him,' he growled. 'You can take him. I'm sick of the sight of him.' Archie was still pretending not to understand and was having difficulty hiding a smile of satisfaction. He had witnessed what had just happened. It echoed the event in Luxor when a conversation had travelled up the chain of command, eventually resulting in the release of Uncle Khali, only this time, he was the uncle to be released.

Later, Ali and Archie were shaking hands by the temple in the Aswan valley.

'Your medallion!' gasped Ali. It's still on the desk by the telephone. I forgot to give it to you.'

'Don't worry,' said Archie. 'You can have it as a gift.'

'No, I'll tell you what,' replied Ali, 'I'll return and bury it here, in front of the ancient gods as an offering. Not that I believe in them, I'm Muslim, but it seems a fitting place for it to rest. I have to go now; I'm back on duty soon. Will you be okay?'

'Oh yes, perfectly fine.' Archie checked his watch, 'I should be meeting up with my old friend Big Bessie very soon. In the meantime, I'll just look inside the temple.'

As Ali drove his jeep back to the army camp, he meditated on the day's momentous events. Before he had picked up his vehicle, he had received another order. He was being transferred to work in Cairo in an intelligence unit responding directly to the man he had spoken to on the telephone. None other than Gamal Abdel Nasser, the President of Egypt.'

CHAPTER THIRTEEN

Lucy was honoured to be sharing a chariot with Queen Nefertiti, although she was also very worried that she would lose her grip and fall. It was certainly an exhilarating ride, although somewhat bumpy. They were going to view the new stela, the celebration of the Pharaoh's power carved into the cliff at the edge of the city.

'The Good God, who rejoices in Ma'at, Lord of Heaven, Lord of earth, the great living orb who illuminates the two banks.' Lucy knew by now that Ma'at was the goddess of harmony, justice, and truth, depicted as a young woman with arms like outstretched wings. Lucy continued to read: 'I shall make the Sun Temple of the Great King's Wife Nefertiti for the Aten, my father, in Akhetaten in this place.' She turned to look at the Queen and whispered, 'Look, Nefi, you've got a mention.'

'Shhh! Don't let anyone hear you call me that in public, but yes, I'm pleased and honoured. My name will be remembered for all time.' Lucy nodded; it was true, perhaps Cleopatra, over a thousand years later, would be more famous, but Nefertiti would be a close second.

As the chariot trundled down the path leading to the centre of the city, Lucy was deep in thought. She remembered the time that she had been in this city before, in 1922, when it was called Amarna, not Akhetaten. She had looked across at this boundary stela when Mary Chubb had been talking about how the archaeologists numbered the houses on their maps. The stela wasn't brightly painted by 1922, and some of the stone had cracked and crumbled away, but Lucy was sure it was the same one.

'Would you mind if I walked the rest of the way?' Lucy called to the Queen. 'My tummy feels very queasy.'

'If you are sure,' replied Nefertiti. She didn't want Lucy being travel sick. Usually, she travelled around the city in this shiny gold chariot with her husband to demonstrate to the people the power and radiance of the Pharaoh. He wouldn't be pleased if someone had thrown up in it! 'Wait until the servants have caught up and one of them can be your guide.'

The servant's name was Omari. It was not a name he liked. It meant 'High Born' and, very aware of his low status, it felt like a cruel joke at his expense. He was tired and hot and wasn't pleased when he was told that he had to climb the hill to look at the stela. He wasn't happy most of the time. He didn't want to leave his family in Karnak and come to this distant city, and he didn't like all the attention that the sun god, Aten, got. He missed the old gods. Now it was going to take him even longer to get back because he had to guide this strange, pale-faced foreign girl.

Lucy was unaware of this seething mass of resentment nestling within the heart of the servant who walked just behind her. She was curious to see the house she had visited with Mary Chubb. She looked over her shoulder at the stela - no, the house was a little way further on.

'This isn't the quickest way,' said Omari.

'Oh, I know. I was just looking for somewhere. That may be it,' Lucy said, pointing to a two-storey house with a crowd of onlookers in front of it.

She asked one of them what was happening.

'It's Nebkef; he's died of the plague. His wife and children are already dead. I don't think he will pass through to the afterlife. They say he wasn't an honest man. They say that he got his money through receiving a cut for turning a blind eye when grave robbers stole the treasures of our ancestors. This house will stay empty now. This plague has killed many of our citizens.' Lucy was almost certain that she had found the place she was looking for. The only way to know would be to go inside and look at the decorative lintel. Whilst Lucy wasn't sure that she could remember the name of the man who had lived in the house she had visited, she was sure she would recognise the painted lintel. For now, it was time to continue her walk back to the Palace with the sullen servant.

***

'Have you had any mosquito bites, James?' asked Robert. 'I've got one on my cheek. I can feel that it's really swollen up; I think it's infected. I don't feel very well. I think I'll take a nap. Don't sit on me.'

It was bright sunlight when Robert closed his eyes, but it was dark when he opened them again. He sat up.

113

'That's odd,' he thought, 'I was lying on a reed mat before, but I appear to be on the ground now.' He waited a while for his eyes to grow accustomed to the dark. 'No, it's not just my bedding that has changed; I've been moved to somewhere different.' He shivered; he was colder than he had been since he was last in England. 'Maybe I'm ill, and I've been taken to a hospital.' He stood up, holding onto the wall for support and then he had a revelation: 'It's cold because I'm in a tunnel; I'm not in a hospital. I'm underground, .' He realised that the tunnel was on a slope. Should he walk uphill, back to ground level, or should he see where this tunnel led? His spirit of adventure drove him downwards.

The tunnel opened out into a large chamber. First, Robert turned left and discovered a room stacked with caskets, carved stools and furniture. There were wheels and the gilded frames from several chariots. 'I seem to have woken up in a subterranean storeroom,' thought Robert. He explored the other direction. He came to another doorway, either side of which two life-sized black and gold figures stood on guard. He passed through to find a room almost filled, from floor to ceiling, with a gigantic, gilded and carved, wooden box. Robert navigated his way around it, only to find yet another storeroom. Then he froze. He wasn't alone.

Robert was used to being invisible and he knew that all he had to do now was breathe quietly and stay still. In front of him stood a young man in his late teens, looking at the contents of the room. Alerted by Robert's presence, he turned around. Robert held his breath.

'Come away from my shrine,' said the young man. Robert didn't move. 'What's that around your neck?' In an involuntary movement, Robert touched the four medallions he was wearing. 'Yes, those. Give them to me. You shouldn't be wearing them.' Robert was astounded; he didn't seem to be invisible anymore because this commanding young man was looking straight at him. 'Give them to me now.'

In a daze, Robert took off the medallions and held them in his outstretched hand. The young man snatched them away, glanced at them, then curled his lip in disgust. Compared to the other treasures Robert could see all around, the youth evidently regarded these as worthless trinkets. He strode over to a white, semi-translucent chest decorated with black text. At each corner stood the statue of a goddess with her arms protectively outstretched. He felt the weight of the lid.

'Come, help,' he commanded, 'It's too heavy for me,' Robert joined him in lifting the lid. Inside, four figures faced each other.

'Finest alabaster,' the young man said, stroking the head of one of them. 'A good likeness, don't you think?' Robert nodded. It dawned on him that the heads of these four figures were stoppers to jars, and he knew what the jars were for. He remembered watching James fill similar jars in the Per Nefer; they contained a mummy's internal organs. Putting that knowledge together with the grandeur of everything around him, Robert concluded that he was in the tomb of somebody very important. The young man placed a medallion around the neck of each of the jars, and then Robert helped him replace the lid of the chest.

'I presume you have come to guide me? It was all rather sudden, so I wasn't sure what to do next.'

'Ermmm,' was all Robert could utter.

'I'm a little disappointed, I had been expecting something much grander, but it's all a bit cramped and cluttered. I had a look around, and there's only one room that has any wall paintings. The tomb should be full of heroic paintings of my life, but..' his voice trailed off and he said mournfully, 'I didn't expect to die so young so maybe no one else expected me to either; it looks like it's all been a bit of a rush. In fact, I don't think this tomb was even intended for me. It's hardly fit for a Pharaoh. I think they have requisitioned it from an administrator or someone much more lowly. I'm going to be a god, don't you know. So, what are you waiting for? Let's go!' Robert followed him out of the room. 'Haven't you forgotten something?' Robert had no idea what was happening and shrugged. 'This. We'll need this,' and the young man handed Robert a papyrus scroll, 'The Book of the Dead.' Then, followed by Robert, he strode out of the room towards a bright light.

'Whoah!' If Robert had been confused before, he was even more confused now. They had left through the same entrance that Robert had used. There should have been a dark tunnel beyond it, but instead they were standing in the open air in a strange landscape. It didn't look like the Egypt Robert had seen before; there were trees, for instance, and tufts of grass waved in the breeze. The ground was sandy, but they weren't in the desert. The sky was a reddish-purple. Robert couldn't tell if the sun was coming up or going down. It turned out that it was doing neither!

'Ah! So this is the Duat,' murmured the young man. He didn't seem surprised to be in this strange place. 'Which way to the Gates of Yaru?'

'Ermmm.'

'Really! What have I done to deserve you as a guide?' He snatched the scroll from Robert and partially unrolled it, read a little, then angrily thrust it back into Robert's hands. 'This way.' He strode off and disappeared behind a dune.

'What have I done to deserve you, you prig!' thought Robert. Just then, there was a cry. Robert climbed to the top of the slope, from where he could see his petulant companion stuck up to his knees in sand. He was sinking.

'Wait!' shouted Robert, 'Don't struggle; it'll make you sink faster. I'll be back.' Robert was good at thinking quickly; it was one reason why he was good at sports. He raced back to the tomb. Taking a gamble, in the hope that he would be back in the same place when he came out, he ran to the first storeroom, grabbed one of the chariot wheels, and to his relief emerged back in that strange eerie landscape. By now, the young man was nearly up to his waist in the quicksand. Checking the ground beneath him was firm, Robert lay on his stomach and held the wheel out for the young man to grab hold of.

It took time and tremendous effort, but eventually Robert hauled his companion to safety. They both lay panting on the sand.

'I suppose I'd better put this back,' said Robert, holding up the wheel, 'I'll be back in a moment.' When he returned, the young man spoke to him:

'Thank you. Without your strength I would not have survived. I have to admit I'm not very strong. My left foot has been weak since I was born and it was made worse when I fell from my chariot during an ostrich hunt.'

'Don't mention it,' replied Robert. Then, thinking of the scroll, he added, 'I have to admit, I'm not very good at reading.' He could read English well enough, but, unlike Lucy, he struggled with all those Ancient Egyptian squiggles.

'Maybe we are together for a reason, then. What shall I call you?'

'Robert. And your name?'

'Oh, I have lots of names. I am the Living Image of Amun, Nebkheperure Tutankhamun.'

'Pleased to meet you. That's quite a mouthful. I'll call you Tut.'

Robert and Tut continued with their journey. Every now and then Tut would unfurl the scroll and read out spells to ward off evil spirits. He didn't seem to have any great sense of direction. He would point to where they needed to go and then promptly walk off in a different direction. Robert would then have to guide him back onto the path. Tut's limp had worsened, so Robert broke a branch off a tree for him to use as a walking stick. After a while, they halted. Facing them was a burning river. It wasn't very wide, but the flames were shooting high into the air. Robert looked downriver in case there was a bridge. He gasped. Walking slowly towards them was a tentacled monster. It was roaring and definitely didn't look friendly.

'We'll go the other way,' said Tut confidently. Robert pulled him back. There was an identical monster approaching from that direction too.

'Are you sure there aren't any spells to help us?' asked Robert. Tut shook his head miserably, 'Lend me your stick for a moment,' said Robert. He thrust the stick down into the water; it was deep. 'Can you swim?'

'Not very well; I tend to sink.'

'Perfect. The flames are on the surface and are mostly on this side of the river. We need to dive in and swim underwater, underneath the flames, right to the other side.'

'But…' said Tut warily.

'There's no time. Those monsters will reach us any moment. Ready? We go together. One, two, three.' The two boys plunged into the water. Robert could have swum faster, but he didn't want to leave Tut behind and kept his eye on him as they struck out for the far bank. Eventually, they had to come up for air. Just a few flames flickered on the surface, but didn't trouble them, and Robert and Tut scrambled up the river bank. The two monsters roared but showed no inclination to follow them.

'Onward!' cried Tut and promptly set off in the wrong direction.

'I thought you said it was this way,' said Robert, pulling him back.

From that point onwards, although long, the journey was less dangerous because The Book of the Dead turned out to contain spells that could dispel any evil creatures that approached them. It never got lighter, nor grew darker as Robert and Tut battled on under that strange, sunless, purple sky.

'At last,' exclaimed Tut in relief, 'The Gates of Yaru are ahead. But first, we must go to the Hall of Two Truths. This way.' After all the wild adventures of their journey through the Duat, as Robert walked through the doors of the building before him, its walls adorned with decoration, he felt relieved to be re-entering civilisation. A tall man with an even taller hat, dressed in a long white robe and sporting a decorative, beaded necklace, was waiting for them.

'Hail to you Osiris, Lord of Eternity, King of Gods, of many names,' chanted Tut.

'So, he's not a man, he's a god,' thought Robert, 'And he's got one of those silly sticky-out beards.'

'I am Osiris, the Lord of the Underworld and Judge of the Dead. I am pleased that you have navigated your way through the Duat. We judges are here today to weigh your sins.' He gestured to an enormous set of scales in the centre of the room. Robert couldn't help noticing the audience. Lining the room was a packed gallery, and Osiris

119

introduced forty-two judges to Tut and Robert. Some he had heard of, like the gods Ra and Isis, but others he found more worrying, like Crusher of Bones, Eater of Entrails and Stinking Face.

'It's time for the negative confessions,' whispered Tut to Robert, as he turned to face the judges.

'Hail, Usekh-nemmt, I have not committed sin.

Hail, Hept-khet, I have not committed robbery with violence.

Hail, Fenti, I have not stolen.

Hail, Am-khaibit, I have not slain men and women.' And so he continued, listing forty-two sins that he hadn't committed. Robert wondered what he would say himself in Tut's position:

'Hail, I have not done my History homework.' No, that didn't sound right.

The judges seemed pleased with Tut's list, and Osiris beckoned him forward to stand by the scales. At the same time, a fierce monster shuffled out from beneath a table. It had the face of a crocodile, the front of a lion and the back of a rhinoceros. 'Welcome, Ammit! Some call him the Devourer, but I prefer to call him the Gobbler,' said Osiris. Then, picking up a white ostrich feather, he said to Tut, 'You know what we must do next if you are to reach the eternal paradise of the Field of Reeds. We must weigh your heart against the feather of truth. Your heart holds all the lies of your past life. If you fail and it's too heavy, then your heart will be eaten by the Gobbler and you will die.'

Robert was taken by surprise and couldn't clearly see what happened next. Osiris seemed to plunge his fist into Tut's chest and bring out his heart. He held it aloft for a moment, then placed it on one side of the scales. It was still beating, and amazingly, Tut stood upright, watching. Then

Osiris put the feather on the other side of the scales, which slowly descended. Tut had passed the test. The judges cheered. Waving to Robert, Tut was led out of the hall to enter through the Gates of Yaru into everlasting paradise.

Robert realised now why the embalmers left the heart in the body. It was for this moment. Presumably, Tut would be reunited with his other body parts later. Also, he understood why Tut's reasoning and sense of direction had been a little wayward. Of course, he didn't have a brain! The embalmers would have poked it out through his nose! Osiris turned to Robert:

'Now it's your turn. To be honest, we weren't expecting two of you. In truth, we didn't really expect him to get through the Duat, but he made it in record time, so we can fit you in too.'

'Ermmm…about the heart thing. Can we skip that bit? I'm rather attached to my heart, literally.' The Gobbler, who had been experiencing hunger pains, pricked his ears up. Maybe not just a heart; he could possibly get to eat a whole body. Robert backed away nervously, then turned and ran. He slammed the door shut behind him to try and hold up the fierce creature. Robert was a fast runner, but there was a big difference between the cross-country routes at school and the terrain he was racing across now. His foot caught on a tree root, and he tumbled down a sand dune, coming to land on his back. At the top of the dune, the deadly monster stood on its hind legs, silhouetted black against the purple sky. The Gobbler jumped, its teeth bared, and everything went black.

CHAPTER FOURTEEN

'Robert! Robert! Robert!' James was shaking Robert's motionless body. He didn't feel dead; he was burning hot, but strangely, he hadn't made a sound for hours. It was morning now. Surely he must wake up soon. James had soaked a cloth in water and wiped it over Robert's face, trying to cool him down. Then suddenly, Robert spluttered into life and sat up.

'Ohhh!' he groaned, 'I can't tell you what a weird dream I've just had.'

'No time anyway,' said James, thinking that other people's dreams were never that interesting. 'We've got to go and see Maya and find out what he wants to do with me.'

***

Archie puzzled over the printouts spread over every surface in the lab. He was sure Big Bessie must have dried out by now. So, it probably wasn't a physical issue. It was more likely a mistake in the coding that he had rewritten. That must have been why he had ended up in the wrong time zone the last time he had used her. He was worried because, if Big Bessie was behaving erratically, how was it affecting Robert, James and Lucy? It seemed Big Bessie had no way of locating where they were.

***

'Are you there, Robert?' asked James.

'Yep! Sure am. You and Big Bessie won't get rid of me that easily!'

'So, we've been blipped to somewhere else. There aren't any landmarks. I wonder where we are?'

'Your clothes have changed, though, you've got some kind of robe on.'

'Do you think we're still in Ancient Egypt? Hold on! What's that noise?' Over the brow of the hill, they saw a horse and then the chariot it was pulling - a very Egyptian - looking chariot.

'It's heading in our direction. Look out!' The horse thundered along the rocky terrain. It seemed out of control, then a chariot wheel hit a boulder and the boys saw the rider flung out of the chariot and land in a crumpled heap. The horse raced on past the twins and they ran in the opposite direction towards the person lying on the ground. It was a boy, perhaps around the same age as them, lying groaning in the dust.

'Are you hurt?' asked James in Egyptian. He could see that the boy had been grazed by the fall, as blood was beginning to ooze from his wounds, but more worryingly, one of the boy's legs was twisted at an unnatural angle.

124

James guessed that the boy was Egyptian by the long white robe, black eyeliner and elaborate blue and gold necklace he was wearing. He guessed right.

'Owwwww! My leg. I can't move it,' he groaned. Robert looked around, seeking help. There was no one. However, he noticed that the horse and chariot had come to a stop in the distance amongst a rocky outcrop.

'I'll go and see if I can bring the chariot back,' he whispered, and he ran towards it. Then he realised that he too was wearing long robes - not the kind of sports kit he was used to. He hitched them up as he ran. Arriving at the chariot, he could see why it had stopped. One of its wheels was jammed between two large rocks.

Robert had very little experience with horses, but he'd once led some to safety from a fire when he was stuck in London in 1824 and, although frightened, they had been obedient. He hoped this one would be as well-trained. Robert had no idea how to make a horse go backwards, so he grabbed hold of the wheel and heaved until he could lift the chariot over the rock that was holding it fast. Then he grabbed hold of the reins and pulled at the horse, so that it turned to face the right direction and he led it back towards James and the injured boy.

They were sitting side by side, watching the horse and chariot approach.

'Look!' said the boy, 'He's is coming back to me. He knows I am the master.' James smiled, he couldn't see Robert either, but he knew he was there. The horse stopped in front of James and the boy.

'But I still ought to punish him for running away with me.'

'Oh no, you can't do that,' replied James quickly. Then, guessing that Robert was still holding the reins, he spoke to the horse. 'I don't know what your name is. I'll call you Horsey-Mac-Horse-Face. Are you listening?' Robert cottoned on fast and, holding on to the horse's bridle, made it nod its head. 'I'm sorry, I don't know your name,' James said to the boy.

'I have five names,' he replied, 'one of them is Nebkheperure.'

'Lord of the forms of Ra,' translated James, 'That's a bit of a mouthful, isn't it? Ra, that's a sun god, so I think I'll call you Sonny. Okay, Horsey-Mac-Horse-Face, are you truly sorry that you ran off with Sonny here? Nod twice if you are.' The horse duly nodded. 'Tell me, Horsey-Mac-Horse-Face, do you recognise Sonny as your master.' The horse nodded twice. 'Finally, Horsey-Mac-Horse-Face, do you think I, James Baxter, am the most talented person in all of the land?' Robert couldn't bear the thought of making the horse nod, and instead, he made it shake its head. Despite the pain he was in, Sonny squealed with laughter.

'Tell him he won't be punished.'

'I think he heard you,' said James, 'Nod three times to say thank you. Good horse! Now, Sonny, I think we had better find help. I can't drive a chariot, but as you've hurt your leg, you will have to sit in it, so I'll lead Horsey on foot.'

James led the horse back in the direction that the chariot had come from. There were no signs of life anywhere. After about thirty minutes, a man on horseback appeared on the horizon. He paused, then lifted a trumpet to his lips and blew a long note.

'Rejoice!' shouted Sonny, 'You've found them!' James gasped as the whole skyline filled with an unbroken line of chariots. After another blast of the trumpet, the army of chariots raced towards them. It was a terrifying sight. The advancing army slowed and halted just before the little group.

'This is the chariot of our King, Nebkheperure,' said a man in the leading chariot. His clothes were more elaborate than those of the men behind him. He wore a leather tunic, on which were fixed bronze rectangles, and a blue helmet-shaped hat. 'How came you by it? Answer now, or I will remove your head from your body.'

'Hello, Horemheb. Don't do that!' shouted Sonny, 'I'm here in the back. James found me. He rescued me!'

'Thanks, Sonny,' said James, 'I'm quite attached to my head. In fact, my head's attached to me. As the song goes, "The head bone's connected to the," Ow!' He didn't get any further because a well-aimed kick on the shin from Robert silenced him. Fortunately, James was no longer the centre of attention. Horemheb leapt from his chariot and prostrated himself on the ground.

'Nebkheperure, who pacifies the Two Lands and satisfied the gods. The strong bull, pleasing of birth. The living image of Amun,' he cried.

'Blow me, isn't a simple "Hi" enough?' whispered James. Robert's reassuring hand rested on James' shoulder.

'Elevated of appearances who satisfied the gods, forgive me, for I failed to keep you safe. I shall punish your guards; I will remove their heads from their bodies.'

'Enough with the removing of heads,' thought James, then he called to Sonny, 'Shall we ask Horsey-Mac-Horse-Face?'

'Good idea! It wasn't the guards' fault; I sneaked forward because I wanted to get closer to the battle but I lost the reins, and the horse bolted. Ask him, James.' To the amazement of the assembled soldiers, the horse shook his head. Sonny grinned, 'That's settled then. Now I want to go home and James will come with me. Also, my horse has just retired from the army. He will lead a life of leisure from now on.'

'Well, that was interesting,' said Robert. He was standing next to James, riding in a chariot led by one of the guards. Sonny was travelling ahead in a more luxurious, horse-drawn carriage, and behind them came the foot soldiers, followed by a long line of prisoners roped together. The Egyptians had been victorious in battle. According to Horemheb, they would all spend the night in a nearby fort and then form a victory parade through the city of Memphis the following morning.

'It looks like our friend, Sonny, is a big deal around here,' said James.

Around twenty-four hours later, James and Robert were sprawled out on cushions, admiring the room allocated to them in the palace. The night in the fort had been so much better than they were used to, but this was on another level. The walls were painted with leaves and birds, a window looked out on ornamental gardens, and a table was piled high with fruit.

The door opened, and a servant entered.

'Nebkheperure, Life, Prosperity, Health, is ready for you now. Follow me,' he said. Before they left, while the servant's back was turned, both Robert and James stuffed a few more grapes into their mouths. Why not? They knew Big Bessie could send them back to a diet of hard, gritty bread at any moment.

'Hello Sonny,' said James cheerily as he walked through the doors into a room even more lavishly decorated than their own. Sonny was seated on an oversized gilded chair decorated with hieroglyphics and paintings of Egyptian gods.

'Actually,' thought Robert, 'it looks more like a throne.'

'People usually bow in my presence,' said Sonny petulantly.

'By all means, what would you like?' replied James, unabashed. First, he clicked his heels and gave a curt nod. Then he bowed from the waist, followed by a more elaborate bow that started with a lot of arm-waving, then, finally, he threw himself full-length on the floor. 'Any of them do?' he asked chirpily. Sonny laughed.

Robert was studying Sonny. He was dressed in a tunic decorated with embroidered patterns. Yesterday his head had been close-shaven but now he wore a black wig with ringlets that reached his shoulders. His injured leg was bandaged. There was something about him that looked familiar. Robert was grasping to remember a dream. It was the shape of Sonny's head, curiously long, and the way his top teeth overhung his bottom ones.

'This may be a stupid question, Sonny,' said James, 'I figured you are pretty important, but are you the king?'

'I most certainly am; I am Lord of the Two lands; I am the Pharaoh.'

As Sonny said this, Robert realised why he looked so familiar and whispered in James' ear:

'It's Tutankhamun!'

'Tell me, James,' said Tutankhamun, 'Where are you from and why are you in Egypt?'

'The first part of your question is easy. I'm from a country far away in the north, called England. As to why I am here, that's a bit more complicated. Let us just say I am a traveller passing through. I sometimes arrive at places quite suddenly and sometimes I have to leave just as quickly. It's not in my hands, so if you find I have gone without saying goodbye, don't take it personally, it's just the way it has to be.'

'I understand. You are like the sun god, Ra. He sails on his boat across the sky from east to west every day, bringing light to the world.'

'Well, yes,' replied James, 'People do say I light up a room when I walk in. I think lighting up the whole world gives me a goal to work towards. So, how does he get back to the east? Does he have to walk?'

'No, a night boat takes him through the underworld, and he is reborn the next day.'

'Ah, like catching an underground train!' laughed James. Then, noticing the Pharaoh looking a little puzzled, he changed the subject: 'Can I ask you something? How come once it was the sun god Aten everybody talked about, but now I don't heard his name at all?'

'You are talking about the days of my father, Akhenaten, when he forced the land to worship only Aten. He closed down temples and destroyed sculptures of other gods. Karnak, in particular, suffered terribly. Now it is my mission to revive the worship of all the old gods and my craftsmen work day and night to restore the temples. I was born Tutankhaten, but I changed my name to Tutankhamun. But enough of serious talk. Do they play senet in this England country you come from?'

'No, I don't think so. I've never heard of it.'

'Really? I thought it was played everywhere. We Egyptians have played it for thousands of years. I shall teach you. Pull that over.' Tutankhamun pointed to what looked like a narrow, black coffee table, which had legs that resembled animal legs and which was mounted on a sledge. The top was divided into thirty ivory squares, in three rows of ten. A drawer in the side of the table contained five blue pieces and five ivory pieces which Tutankhamun laid out in a row, alternating the colours. Robert whispered to James as his brother fetched a chair.

'I think you should let him win.' The basic rules were fairly simple and had some similarities to the game of Snakes and Ladders. Players moved the pieces around the board according to the number on the thrown dice, and the first person to get all their pieces off the board won. Actually, they were not dice, but rather four throwing sticks, black on one side and white on the other, and scores were calculated according to which way up they landed. There were some complications, and somehow Tutankhamun always seemed to benefit from them.

'Four whites, that means I get an extra throw. You see that square with the hieroglyphics that I have landed on? That's the House of Rebirth; it means I get an extra go. See, I've landed on you: it means you have to go back to the square I came from. Oh no, you can't land on me because I have two pieces next to each other.' And so it went for the rest of the morning. Eventually, James knew all the rules, not that it did him any good. It wasn't a case of letting Tutankhamun win. Even though a lot of luck was involved, James lost every game; the boy king was too good.

'I think you need some more practice,' laughed Tutankhamun, 'I have many senet sets. I will ask a servant to put a small travelling set in your room. You can have it as a gift.'

***

'Do you know, I could get used to this,' said James as they strolled around the Palace's ornamental lake. They were on their way from the Royal Apartments to a building where official business was carried out. 'It certainly beats going to school. We've done nothing other than laze around, play senet and eat the finest food. If it wasn't for the problem of you being invisible and not knowing how long we have to cure you, then I could put up with this for a good while longer. I miss Lucy of course, but at least she's in a palace too, with Queen Nefertiti.'

'Is she Tut's mum or his Aunt?' asked Robert.

'I don't know. Pharaohs have several wives, and the children are brought up by a nurse or guardian, their Menat, so it's all very complicated.'

The complex nature of relationships was emphasised when, as they entered Tut's room, a girl, perhaps the same age as them, swept out, followed by an entourage.

'You've just missed my wife, the Queen, Ankhesenamen,' said Tut brightly. 'She just popped in to see how my leg is healing.'

'Your wife!' gasped James, 'How old are you?'

'I am fourteen,' said Tut proudly, 'I've been married since I became Pharaoh when I was nine.'

'We are fourteen too,' said James.

'We?'

'Oh, me and my twin brother. Erm…I haven't seen him for a while.'

'I know; families are complicated, especially Royal ones. We only usually see each other for official ceremonies. Speaking of which, you'll have to disappear for a while. My Vizier, Ay, is coming to see me soon.'

'Aye, Aye, Captain' said James with a salute.

'He's been one of my advisors since I became King,' said Tut gloomily, 'It's not so much advice I get from Ay and Horemheb; instructions are what they give. You may think it's an easy life being a Pharaoh, but it's one long round of meetings and ceremonies and yet more meetings.'

***

James and Robert, sitting on an ornamental wall, watched the imposing figure of Ay stride away from the Palace, having finished his meeting with the Pharaoh. They could understand why Tutankhamun would find him intimidating.

'The thing is,' said Robert, 'I can't help feeling sad about the fact that we know he is going to die young.'

'I know,' replied James, 'But it happened and there is nothing that we can do about it. We can't let on that we know. All we can do is try and help him with the here and now.'

'Let's go and see him, Mind you, I don't feel there's a lot I can do to contribute, James. Unless you want me to go and get Horsey-Mac-Horse-Face.'

***

'Hello Tut,' said James cheerily, 'Have you noticed that I've started calling you Tut instead of Sonny now?'

'Very reverential,' replied Tut, wryly.

'Cheer up! What's happened?'

'It's Ay; he's just given me this.' Tut held up a papyrus scroll, 'I've got to give a speech to the most influential men in Egypt. The courtyard will be packed, and I'm no good at that kind of thing.'

'Don't worry!' I'll help you learn it. I'm good at learning lines.'

'It's not learning the speech that's the problem, it's me.'

'What do you mean?' asked James

'Well, just look at me. My teeth stick out. I have problems walking and often have to use a stick. My voice is strange, don't tell me you haven't noticed. It's on account of me being born with a hole in the roof of my mouth. I get out of breath easily. I get self-conscious, I suppose. I'm

133

not like other people.'

'Rubbish!' replied James,' You've only said one thing that isn't absolute tosh; it's true, you aren't like other people, but that's because you aren't supposed to be like everyone else - you're a living god, for goodness sake. You've got to celebrate the differences. I can help, this is my world. I'm your man.'

'Thank you, but I'm not sure I can change this speech.'

'Oh, I'm not talking about the words. You Egyptians have your own way with words, all that repetition for example - May the god grant favour to your house, may the god grant favour to your wife, may the god... and all that kind of stuff. No, what I'm talking about is stagecraft. I'll give you the time it takes me to walk to the end of the gardens and back for you to have a read through, and then we'll be good to go.'

Thirty minutes later, Robert and James were back. Robert settled himself down at the back of the room to watch a master at work.

'First of all, tell me, how's your leg? Good. I'm glad it's only a sprain. How big's the stage or platform? Okay. So, I presume you're going to be carried in one of those chairs on poles, Yes? So let's take it from the moment you get out of the chair... And, action! Woah, Woah, Woah! You can't just get out of the chair and start talking. What kind of entrance is that? Where's your walking stick? Take this one. Now, when you get out of the chair, just stand for a moment. Spread your legs more, puff out your chest, chin up, that's it. Kingly. Now I'll tell you what I think will be happening right now, everyone will be face down on the floor. That's no good. How can they be impressed by you if they can't see higher than your sandals? Give them a moment to show respect, then make a gesture to tell them to get up. Make sure there are a few people in the crowd who will know when to make the first move. The others will follow. Now, everyone is up and cheering; again, get the guys you've planted in the audience to start it. Give it a second, stretch your arms out; your cane will exaggerate the move. Now hold the stick above your head with two hands. That's it! Milk it. Now move forward, check out the crowd, hold your walking stick in one hand and point with the other. Point to different parts of the crowd with a smile as if to say, "Hi, so glad you can make it!" People will think you mean them personally. So, you've arrived; now you can start your speech...Woah, Woah, Woah! You're going too fast. Say a line, then look up, look to the left, look to the right, remember the people at the back. Legs a little wider, take up more space, come on, own that stage. That's good. Now, wait, you've just mentioned the Sun God, right? I'm presuming it's daytime. So, one thing you can say about Egypt is the sun's going to be shining, right? So use your cane; it's a prop, so point to the sun with it. Now, here's a move you may have to practise, throw it high in the air with one hand and catch it with the other, then you can do that two-handed pose again. As you lower your cane, make a gesture to quieten the crowd. Looking around the audience and nodding is a good move here. Yeah, baby, you've got it! Now, when you've finished, throw your walking stick high in the air and let it land behind you. Actually, you'd better have a servant catch it - there's a lot of gold on that stick and you don't want to break it; I'll catch it this time. Now do the arms-outstretched pose again. You don't need the stick because two servants are going to come and lift you onto their shoulders. Just imagine it, your arms still out wide, majestic, victorious, and them carrying you back to your chair. Magnificent. Ladies and Gentlemen, The King has left the building!'

CHAPTER FIFTEEN

Robert and James had hoped that they would be able to see the show, but Big Bessie had other ideas. They had spent most of the previous day either playing senet or watching Tut rehearse his moves. Tut was getting so confident that his act wouldn't have looked out of place in The Rock and Roll Hall of Fame. When they settled down to sleep that night, Robert made sure he was holding the travelling senet set. He guessed Big Bessie would come calling. Sure enough, before they had fallen asleep, he and James felt that familiar sensation of moving through time and space, and found themselves back in Karnak on the roof of the building where they usually slept.

'Ah well. It was nice while it lasted. These reed mats are a lot harder than the Palace beds, aren't they?' said

James, trying to get comfortable.

'At least the senet set has come with us,' replied Robert.

'What are we having for breakfast? I know, don't tell me...bread!

***

Robert and James were in the temple at Karnak, waiting to see Maya. 'Uh oh, here's Big Bessie again,' James yelled. His words were lost in the vortex as the familiar sensation of being sucked through time enveloped him. Both brothers held their breath and waited to arrive at their destination. What surprised them was that, when they arrived, they were totally submerged in deep, cold water. Robert let out a gasp and most of the air in his lungs bubbled up to the surface. He could see that both he and his brother were stuck, their legs trapped between rocks. James struggled with the rock covering his foot, but it was too large and heavy for him to move and he couldn't get at it from the right angle. Robert managed to wriggle free and had no choice other than to head for the surface, where he took a big gulp of air, then flipped over and swam down to where James was feebly trying to free himself. He had almost spent all his breath. Robert braced himself with his back against a large boulder, his hands clutching it to prevent himself from rising to the surface and pushed with both feet against the rock that was holding James fast. It was tough, but with a tremendous effort, he managed to shove the rock aside, grab hold of James under the arms and kick his way upwards.

James was unconscious. Robert swam with him to a rocky ledge and hauled him out of the water. Fortunately, Robert had passed his life-saving qualifications, and without panicking, he immediately followed the drill that he had

138

been taught. James coughed and spluttered back to life.

'Thank you, Big Bessie,' he groaned. 'If you thought I needed a bath, why didn't you just ask?'

For twenty minutes, the boys lay on their backs, staring up at the blue sky while they recovered from their ordeal.

'It's a good job I wasn't the one who was stuck,' said Robert. 'You wouldn't have been able to see me. I'm going to go back in. When I was moving the rock, I saw one of our medallions. I didn't have time to pick it up. It would be a shame to leave it there. I'll take these others off.' Robert removed the rest of the medallions from around his neck, laid them on the ledge, and dived back into the water. He was back in a moment, holding his prize aloft as though he had just won it in the Olympics. He laid it next to the others. It hadn't had time to turn invisible yet, and the ones he had just taken off were beginning to appear.' 'Robert!' exclaimed James. 'Do you see what I see? Count them.' Four medallions, not three, lay side by side on the rock. 'That can only mean one thing; Uncle Archie has been here! I hope he is alright. I hope he hasn't drowned.'

'I'll tell you something else,' said Robert, 'Before we came here, I was wearing a white skirt and sandals. Now I've got jeans and trainers on, and what does it say on this tee shirt?'

'It says "Live Aid, Saturday 13th July 1985, Wembley Stadium."

'Okay, that's pretty useful. The date has to be after then. Where are we anyway? It's too hot to be Wembley. Are we still in Egypt?' Both boys turned around and stood silent for a moment, open-mouthed.

'We've been here before.' said James. 'Only there wasn't a massive big lake here then. We are at the Ramses temple where Maya sent me to make offerings to the gods.'

'This is just weird. It's like Big Bessie has blipped us into a different time zone,' said Robert, placing all four medallions back around his neck, 'Why are we here?' This must have acted as a signal for Big Bessie to act because, suddenly, she made her move and they weren't there anymore.

***

'Hmmm! That didn't work,' said Archie to himself, puzzling over his code. He had set Big Bessie to take him to Egypt, but to return ten seconds later, before he had a chance to get into trouble. He didn't want to risk getting arrested again! He didn't have enough time to work out where he was; it looked like Egypt, but he seemed to be wearing a skirt, which told him that Big Bessie had sent him a long way back in time. It wasn't that often that his knobbly knees and brilliant white legs got an airing. Not a pretty sight!

***

'Do we have to go to Akhetaten?' complained Asim.

'We have no choice,' replied Maya. 'Our world is getting smaller. The Pharaoh has seized our lands to provide wealth for his god. My spies tell me that he has directed thirteen thousand men and women to service his temple at Per Aten, here in Karnak. Our temples have to pay taxes directly to him. We cannot risk annoying him, or he may tear down the statues of our gods and deface our temple walls. '

'But another festival!'

'I know, firstly he had that Sed Festival, normally held to celebrate thirty years on the throne, after just three years, and now this, the Festival of Tribute. Rulers from all over the world will bring gifts and subjugate themselves before him. We have to be there.'

'And what are we to do with that red-headed boy?' asked Asim.

'He is like a bad spirit. From the moment I first set eyes on him, our troubles began. The problem is I swore to the Queen that I would not cause him harm.'

'Might I make a suggestion, Oh revered High Priest? Just like your family, most of mine are priests, except one. Do you know Potasimto? He is a General. A ruthless killer. He is returning from war with the Hittites.'

'I've never met him.'

'Good, then there is no connection between you and him. We need a little more time; perhaps you could send the boy on another long journey. North this time, to Imentet?'

Asim didn't need to wait for a reply. The smile on Maya's face was all the approval he needed.

***

Hello, hello, we're back in the temple in Karnak,' said Robert, 'I wonder if you've missed your meeting with Maya. It might be a little complicated trying to explain where we've been.' The answer came by way of three claps from a shadowy alcove. Maya was ready for James now. Ten minutes later, he had dismissed him.

'I wonder where Imentet is?' wondered James.

'For the most part, directions are pretty simple. We know it's north, so all we've got to do is walk down to the river and turn left,' said Robert, confidently.

***

'Maybe this is the problem,' thought Archie, as he typed more code into Big Bessie's data bank. He had a nagging feeling that he was over-complicating things and making them worse. Still, it was worth a try!

141

***

James and Robert walked down to the river to wait for a boat to take them north.

'Let's have a spot of lunch. What delicacies do we have today?' asked Robert. He knew what James would say, though.

'Bread!'

Then Big Bessie intervened. The view changed, but they were still holding their lunch, so James and Robert each took a bite. To their surprise, what started out as the usual dry, coarse, sandy bread turned into something much tastier. Big Bessie had added a hummus filling. They ate quickly in case she changed it back again, then, licking their lips, they tried to figure out where they were.

'If I'm not mistaken, we've been here before,' said James. 'I think we are back in Nubia, but something very, very big is missing.'

'You're right,' said Robert, staring at the gigantic hole that had been cut into the side of the cliff. 'Someone has stolen the temple!'

'Incredible, you can't leave anything around here, put it down for a second and someone will nick it. Wardrobe analysis, please, Robert.' James struck a pose like a fashion model.

'This is what today's hip young things are wearing,' replied Robert, 'Starting at the feet, we have some very dusty, open-toed sandals just peeping out from a pair of groovy, red, flared trousers and topped with a tie-dyed tee shirt, not to mention a rather fetching plaited headband.' James looked down at himself.

'I'll tell you what it reminds me of. Do you remember when we went back to London in 1966? These are a lot like the clothes the hippies were wearing.'

'Yes, you're right, so we're in the 1960s. What is Big Bessie playing at? Why here, why now?'

As if in answer, a figure appeared on the clifftop above them, descending down a rocky path. It was a teenaged girl; her clothes were dusty and ragged, a scarf covered her hair, and she was sobbing loudly. Then they heard a shriek, and saw the girl lose her footing on a patch of shingle, slide and roll down the path to rest close to where Robert and James were standing. They rushed forward and James helped her to sit up. She was sobbing ever more loudly now.

'Are you hurt?' asked James. There was no answer. Then James realised that she was unlikely to understand him because he had spoken in English. He waited.

'Peace be upon you,' said the girl, trying to struggle to her feet. It had taken James and Robert a few seconds to adjust, but now they understood what she was saying and, having been to the same region before, albeit thousands of years earlier, they figured she must be descended from the Nubians.

'Let me help,' said James, giving her his hand. The dark-skinned, dark-haired girl looked astonished that this red-headed, pale-skinned, freckled boy could speak her language. She wrapped her scarf back around her head, for it had slipped off during her fall, and stared at him.

'Why are you here?' she asked, 'It's a protected zone.'

'Then why are you here?' replied James, not knowing how best to answer her question. It was then that she started to cry again. James didn't know what to do. He reckoned that she was Muslim and therefore would not welcome being touched by a man, so he waited, hands clasped together, and looked at her with concern. Eventually, she started to talk and, once she had started, the words came tumbling out.

'It's my Grandfather. He's gone missing and I've searched for three days for him. This is my last hope. I'm wondering if he has gone back to our old house. If he has, I don't know how he found the strength to walk there; he is very ill. He had never wanted to leave his birthplace; he kept saying that he wished to die in his own bed, and then one night he disappeared.'

'Can't you telephone someone in the village,' asked James. She looked at him as though he were stupid, then, deciding to make allowances as he was so obviously a foreigner, she explained the situation.

'Nobody lives in the village; we were all moved out to new homes because the whole valley is to be flooded. The government is building a huge dam and the waters are rising by the hour. I must go now while I can.'

'We can…I mean…I can come with you. Maybe that's why I'm here. Lead on! I'm James by the way.'

'My name is Alia.'

Thirty minutes later, they arrived at a village of brightly-coloured houses, many decorated with scenes of palm trees, birds and animals. The windows and doorways were painted in contrasting colours and the roofs were rounded. Once, the village might have been described as "nestling by the edge of the Nile", now they were wading through knee-deep water to reach it.

'It's very pretty,' said James as they splashed along. Robert was taking care to walk directly behind James so he wouldn't be detected.

'Soon, it will all be gone,' said Alia sadly. 'You should see the village that the government moved us to, we are squashed into tiny houses. They hadn't even started building some of them, and worst of all, we are so far away from the Nile. The river has always been the lifeblood of our community and now we have been cut off from it! This is my grandfather's house, the yellow one.' Alia and James entered through the open doorway.

'Grandfather,' gasped Alia, and she rushed over to him. A small, thin man was lying on his back on a table in the middle of the room. His eyes were closed, and he was breathing heavily.

'It's Alia,' his granddaughter cried, touching his hand. His eyes remained shut, but he reached out a hand and squeezed hers. Then he held up his other hand and offered something to her. It was a small, carved, stone doll.

'Oh, Grandfather, you do know it's me. I used to play with this when I was little. I didn't realise we had left it here.' The old man's breathing grew louder, he squeezed Alia's hand once more, and then all went quiet and still.

There were a few moments of silence, then Alia burst into tears. James stood motionless; he realised that he had just witnessed someone die.

'Verily we belong to Allah, and truly to Him shall we return,' Alia whispered.

'I'll leave you for a moment,' said James, and he went outside. Robert touched his shoulder.

'I saw,' he whispered.

After a few minutes James returned to comfort the weeping Alia.

'He knew it was his time,' she said, 'He got his wish, to die here in the house where he was born. But what am I to do? He can't stay here to be washed away and eaten by crocodiles. Our custom is that he should be buried within three days. I can go and get help, but I don't know if I'll be here in time.'

'I have a suggestion, why don't you go and get help,

and I will carry your grandfather back to where we first met you. I'm stronger than I look.' This rather embellished the facts; James wasn't any stronger than he looked, but he had Robert waiting in the wings. 'Go now, quickly.'

'Are you sure?'

'Yes. You asked why I was here. Maybe this is why. Go! Hurry, and don't look back. You wouldn't want to remember him this way.' The twins waited until the sound of Alia splashing through the water died away, then went back inside the house.

'Do you know, there was a time when I might have felt a bit squeamish about what we are about to do, but after preparing mummies in that tent, I don't have a problem with it at all,' said James. 'Which end do you want?'

'I don't mind. We could start by carrying him on this table until the path gets too steep, but let's get a move on. I'm not too keen on being a crocodile's dinner. He might not see me, but he could probably smell me and eat me. He might even be a descendant of the one we met before around here and be holding a three-thousand-year grudge!

It took the boys an hour to get back to where they first met Alia. They had turned the table over and pulled it like a sledge most of the way, before leaving it behind a bush and carrying Alia's grandfather the last few paces. All in all, they felt it was as dignified a journey as they could manage. They laid him in the space where the stolen temple had been and stretched out to recover.

It was beginning to get dark when they heard a commotion. A group of people, led by Alia and carrying torches, was coming down the path. Alia rushed to her grandfather, almost as though she was reassuring herself that this was all really happening. Then she turned to James.

'How can I ever thank you? You must be so strong!'

'No worries, I work out. Ouch!' The last exclamation was because Robert had kicked him on the shin. 'Little twinge,' he said ruefully, rubbing his leg.

'Can I ask you something? Would you take this?' Alia held out the little carved doll. 'If I keep it, I will always remember this day when I see it, and as you said, this isn't how I want to remember Grandfather. I don't mind if you don't hang on to it. I just don't want to throw it away.' James took the figurine with a nod and a smile, then Alia returned to the group of people clustered around her grandfather, one of whom was the local Iman, who uttered the same words Alia had spoken earlier:

'Verily we belong to Allah, and truly to Him shall we return.'

Alia would always feel guilty that she hadn't said goodbye to James, but she understood that he might have wanted to slip away quietly. In fact, even if James and Robert had wanted to hang around, Big Bessie had other ideas.

***

Lucy thought back over the past few, eventful days. There were many things to worry about. Firstly she was separated from her brothers; they were in Thebes, while she was living in the gleaming white city of Akhetaten. Secondly, what had happened to Uncle Archie and Big Bessie? She knew that you could only travel back to the lab with Big Bessie from where you had arrived. Her brothers had only ever arrived at Karnak when travelling to Egypt, but she had also travelled from this city, Amarna. Something had gone wrong and they had all ended up over two thousand years in the past. Lucy paused outside the compound of the large townhouse; the other thing to worry about was that today would be her first day at work. She had told Nefertiti that she liked drawing and painting, and now here she was at the house of Bek, the master sculptor, where she was going to start her apprenticeship.

She was shown through to a workshop in the courtyard and was immediately put to work decorating a large ceramic pot, copying the design from another one. These were pieces intended for the temple, and Lucy was taught to use various techniques. The pot was first dipped in a glaze, then Lucy scratched patterns through the glaze before applying further decoration with a brush. She was pleased with her results but was even more gratified when Bek nodded his approval.

'You have a talent for this,' he said. 'They are almost identical.' Lucy thought back to her last art tutorial at school when her teacher had scolded her for copying.

'I'd like to see how you would get on here, Monsieur Henri Pastiche!'

Lucy spent her evenings in the royal palace with the other women and children. By now, she had met Nefertiti's daughters, Meri, Meket and Ankhes. Although the Queen was genuinely fond of them, she had little to do with their upbringing. The Menat, the royal nursemaid and teacher, took care of that. Nefertiti's priority was to fulfil her duties as Chief Royal Wife. Bathing, having her servants anointing her body with oils and perfumes and, of course, applying her black eye-liner, all took time. The Pharaoh had another wife, Kiya, but Nefertiti didn't like talking about her to Lucy. There was obviously some jealousy there. However, Nefertiti was pleased to point out that Kiya, unlike herself, was never depicted in paintings wearing a crown. Nefertiti was definitely the favoured wife. Once a day, Nefertiti and the Pharaoh drove through the city streets in a gold chariot before going to the temple, where Akhenaten would make offerings to the sun god.

Lucy was pleased that having a friend in the Queen had led to an improvement in one specific aspect of her life. Nefertiti had instructed her servants to keep Lucy supplied with boiled water from the Nile to drink. Everyone else in Egypt seemed to drink thick, cloudy beer. Although it wasn't very alcoholic and was probably quite nutritious, it tasted awful. Lucy had just left the main room of the palace, where everyone gathered to rest and talk, to fetch herself some more water from the clay bottles in the store, when she heard a familiar voice.

'Hello Lucy,' Her heart soared.

'Robert!! How did you find me?'

'It was fairly easy, I just walked down all the widest roads. I figured that they would lead to the palace, and then the presence of all the guards and soldiers told me I was in the right place.'

'What are you doing here?'

'Just passing through. The High Priest keeps giving James errands to run. He wants him out of the way, I think. We're on a boat, sailing to somewhere called Imentet to take an offering. He said James would know he was in the right place because there are pyramids there. I'm hoping to climb one.'

'Pyramids! I think they're in a place we call Giza now.'

'Anyway, we just wanted to let you know that we are okay. How's life with you?'

'All the better for hearing your voice. Physically my life is fine, privileged really. I spend my day's painting, I'm well-fed, and I have somewhere safe to sleep. There are some dark times, though, when I worry about you two, and how Uncle Archie will find us again.'

'Keep your pecker up, Lucy. Tell me, has Big Bessie taken you anywhere lately?'

'No, I've been here the whole time. Why do you ask?'

'Oh, I was just wondering.' Robert decided that he wouldn't tell her about how Big Bessie had been blipping them around time and space just yet. It would only give her something else to worry about. 'I'd better be getting back to the boat. James will be worried if I'm away too long.'

'Do you want to take a bottle of boiled water back with you?'

'Oh, heaven! Have you tasted the beer?'

CHAPTER SIXTEEN

Lucy wasn't in a hurry to leave the studio. She had finished her working day, but she wanted to ask Bek something. A layer of wet clay covered the table, and Lucy idly doodled in it with a stick. She had been thinking about Robert's recent visit, so she decided to draw a caricature of him. First, Lucy drew a large head, with full thick lips, then a body, not quite in proportion, followed by a pair of very long legs. As she stepped back to admire her work, Bek entered the room.

'Sorry,' said Lucy, noticing Bek looking at what she had drawn on the table, 'I was waiting to ask you something. I'll clear it up.'

'No, wait.' Bek studied it for a while, 'This is interesting. Here we are living in this new city. The Pharaoh has changed the religion of this country, but now he wants a new style of art. Something that people will associate with him and be a break from the old ways. So what have you done here?' Bek drew marks along the top and down the side of Lucy's drawing. 'I see, normally our figures fit into a grid of eighteen squares, but yours is twenty. Interesting! A few adjustments, like making his belly bigger to show he's not short of food, and I think we have something here. What was it you wanted to ask me?'

'It's this pot. It's got a crack in it, so it won't be any good for the temple. Do you mind if I have it to practise on?'

'No, not at all. Now, I'll just make a record of this.' Bek placed a piece of papyrus over Lucy's work, pressed down and made a print. Then they both left the workshop, happy for different reasons.

***

'Ow!' James and Robert had landed in a heap on the dark and rocky floor.

'Where are we?' asked James.

'I don't know. I think Big Bessie has been having one of her hiccups again. It does seem familiar, though. As though I've been here before, but in a dream.'

'Look! There's a torch burning down there. Let's go see.' James got to his feet and walked down a tunnel towards the light, presuming that Robert would follow close behind. Robert did follow, but slowly, for he had an unsettling sense of déjà vu. James turned the corner just as the fog in Robert's brain cleared.

'Surely not. I can't go through that again.' He was just about to call out to James when he heard his brother speaking.

'Hi, guys. I don't suppose you can tell me where we

are and how we get out of here?' Then Robert heard the sound of men shouting. He began to run and was just in time to see three men grab his brother and drag him further down to where the tunnel opened out. Robert knew where this was alright. He was back in the tomb of Tutankhamun, but whilst he recognised the room, it was in complete disarray. They had stumbled upon a group of men who were ransacking it. Grave robbers!

'How did you get here?' demanded one of the men.

'I...I...I don't know. I just found myself here,' stammered James.

'What shall we do with him?' asked another.

'Tie him up and gag him. I don't think our voices will carry up to the surface, but we can't take the risk. We mustn't let the guards hear us. We'll decide later. I don't know how he got past our lookout. Get on with your work and remember, only things we can carry easily, like jewellery. Perhaps we can come back for the rest another day. Break down that sealed door. There are bound to be more treasure through there. We haven't found the royal mummy yet.'

Robert was in a dilemma. First and foremost, he wanted to save his brother, but he could see that even if he could untie the ropes that bound him, the chances of James being able to get past the strong, burly men who stood between him and freedom were remote. Strangely, Robert also felt a responsibility towards Tut. He hated the fact that they were rifling through the possessions that were intended to help him in the afterlife. He tiptoed over to where his brother was lying.

'I'll get help,' he whispered. James nodded. One of the robbers turned his head but then, seeing nothing, continued with his task of wrapping a stash of gold rings in a cloth.

Robert crept out of the room and then sped along the tunnel to the surface.

Robert was on the alert because the grave robbers had mentioned a lookout, but they had also mentioned there might be guards. The lookout was very visible, almost blocking his way at the top of the steps. He squeezed past him, but then, guards? Where would he find guards? He might run off and search in completely the wrong direction. Then he realised what to do. He would have to be 'the guards'. Robert picked up one of the rocks that had been used to hide the entrance to the tomb and he tossed it as far as he could, making the lookout jump up to investigate. Then, at the top of his voice, Robert shouted into the tunnel:

'The guards are coming! The guards are here!' This confused the lookout. He didn't recognise the voice, but he wasn't prepared to hang around to investigate. The punishment for grave-robbing was death and a painful one at that. When Robert was sure that the lookout was gone, he ran back into the tunnel, yelling:

'Stop, in the name of the Pharaoh!' It sounded a bit corny, but it seemed to have the desired effect because he heard shouting from below. Aware that he might get knocked over when the grave robbers rushed to escape, he turned and ran back to the entrance, climbed out, and stood to one side watching with satisfaction as the criminals scrambled out into the night air and fled in the direction of the river. Although some of them were carrying booty, he was pleased to see that others were empty-handed.

'Stop in the name of the Pharaoh!' laughed James as Robert untied him.

'I couldn't think of anything else. We don't even know who the Pharaoh is,' replied Robert, 'But I figured we are still in Ancient Egypt because you're still wearing a skirt. Come on, let's go and find a guard and you can tell them about the break-in. You don't have to admit you were down here - just tell them you saw men running towards the Nile.'

***

Lucy slipped quietly out of the palace gates, nodding at the guard, who recognised her. It was unusual for a female to leave at this time of night, but it wasn't his place to interfere. Shortly afterwards, he saw someone else leave. It was a particularly sour individual called Omari. Maybe it was his job to keep his eye on the young foreign girl.

This wasn't that far from the truth, but Omari hadn't been told to follow Lucy; it was his own idea. He had taken a dislike to Lucy's presence in the palace and, seeing her leave alone, he had decided on the spur of the moment to follow her. He couldn't think where she was going or what was in the bag she carried. There was a full moon and he kept to the shadows so that she would not see him.

Lucy walked quickly. It wasn't the first time she had travelled this route; she had been this way only the day before. She arrived at her destination and, just as she had noticed previously, the door to the property was slightly ajar. She looked around in all directions to check no one was around, then stealthily squeezed through the door and disappeared out of sight. However, hiding behind a wall, Omari had observed her and was astonished to see her go into Nebkef's house -the house which had been deserted after all the occupants had died of the plague.

Inside, Lucy was trembling. She had thought long and hard about whether she dared do this. It wasn't just the act of breaking into someone's house. It was also the risk of catching the plague. In the end, her sense of reason

155

prevailed. Lucy figured that the plague was probably transferred by touch or by breath, and so was unlikely to be waiting for her in an empty house. In any case, maybe her ancestors would have built up a natural immunity over the generations. It was worth taking the risk; she couldn't think of any other way to change her circumstances.

There were clay tiles on the floor. Lucy hadn't expected that. They hadn't been there when she was in this house in 1922. She peered around to orientate herself and then groped her way over to a corner of the room and unpacked the sack she was carrying; it contained some tools from the artist's workshop and the pot with a crack in it, now decorated, glazed and fired with her own designs.

Lucy's eyes had by now grown accustomed to the dark and, prising several of the tiles up, she started to dig in the compacted sand. The more she dug, the easier it became, and eventually, she had created a hole big enough to bury her pot. Then she backfilled the hole, replaced the floor tiles and scooped up the excess soil into the sack. Finally, she used her feet to scatter any sand she had spilled and placed a chair over the area where she had been working. Satisfied, but still trembling with nervous energy, Lucy left the house and emptied the sack on some waste ground a little way down the road. Then clutching her artist's tools, she returned to the palace. Job done!

From behind the wall, Omari had been watching Lucy, and now he crept over to see what she had emptied out of the sack. He hadn't dared get any closer to the plague house, so he had no idea what she had been doing in there. Finding that Lucy had discarded a pile of sand, Omari was utterly dumbfounded. He fished about in it, hoping for treasure, but there was none. What was she up to? He was going to have to keep his eye on her.

***

Robert and James were getting used to the slow pace of life as they sailed north up the river to Imentet.

'I've been thinking,' said Robert, 'You know that little doll thing that the girl whose grandfather had died gave us when we blipped forward in time?'

'Yes.'

'Well, I'm a little fed up of carrying it around. I tucked it into my waistband, but it's a bit uncomfortable, so I think I'm going to put it on top of a pyramid.'

'Cool! It will be like our offering.'

The following day, having left the boat, they were staring up at the pyramids, open-mouthed in amazement.

'I wasn't expecting this. I don't think I'll be climbing up there!' gasped Robert. Instead of the stepped, sandy-coloured pyramids familiar to them, these three pyramids were a smooth, dazzling white, each topped with a golden cone. 'Plan B then.'

'Maybe I should hand this offering over to the temple now. I reckon it will be dark in an hour or so,' said James. The sun was low in the sky and cast a long, dark, triangular shadow behind each pyramid.

'You go and do that,' replied Robert, 'I know just where to put this. I'm going to bury it at the tip of that shadow.'

James walked to the building that Maya had instructed him to visit. The Mortuary Temple served the largest pyramid and was sited along a canal leading to the Nile. Both boys had been surprised by how many buildings there were around the pyramids. They had expected the pyramids to be standing alone in the middle of the desert, but there were rows of rectangular structures built all around them. The priest in the mortuary temple, who gladly took the offering from James, explained that the smaller buildings were the tombs of workers who had constructed the pyramids. The priest gave the impression that he was serving in a forgotten outpost. It was over a thousand years since the Pharaohs had built the pyramids; now, the tombs of the Pharaohs had been relocated to the Valley of the Kings, further south, where their tombs could be hidden from grave robbers. Nature, in the form of the sun and the wind, was doing its best to destroy Imentet's monuments and buildings.

'In two weeks, it will be the beginning of the flood season,' said the priest with satisfaction, 'Then the farmers won't be able to work in the fields and I shall have a workforce. The Sphinx is getting covered by sand. It needs digging out and requires a fresh coat of paint.'

James returned to find his brother. Actually, it was more a case of standing in the shadow of the pyramid and waiting for Robert to find him.

'Hiya, that was more difficult than I thought it would be. The ground is quite rocky here; I suppose it has to be if a pyramid is going to sit on it, but luckily there was a crack, and I managed to poke our little dolly friend into it. Where now?'

'The ancient city of Memphis is nearby. We were there with Tut but he hasn't even been born yet! I suppose there's a vague chance that Big Bessie could scoop us up and drop us off in Memphis, Tennessee. Then we could get a burger,' said James, licking his lips.

'Unlikely,' sighed Robert.

'But maybe we should just head back to the river and find a boat. I think High Priest Maya will be missing us!'

***

'Aagh! Numbskull!' cried Archie, slapping himself

around the head to emphasise the point. He was staring at Big Bessie's code. The hex sign for a female is U+2640, and for a male, it's U+2642, but Archie realised that, in his panic to get Big Bessie working, he had typed U-2642. A minus instead of a plus could have caused untold damage. 'More haste less speed,' he muttered. This mistake meant that the boys might have been bounced around in time. At least Lucy would have stayed put.

CHAPTER SEVENTEEN

'Hello Lucy,' said Nefertiti, 'I haven't seen much of you lately; I've been so busy getting prepared for the festival. How is the world of art?'

'Hello, Nefi. Life, Prosperity, Health. I've been enjoying it, thanks. Bek says we've developed a whole new style that will forever be associated with you and the Pharaoh. Also, I'm glad to hear that many more paintings are being produced that show your whole family - you, Akhenaten and your three children.'

'Yes, I just love new things. Speaking of which, I am sure child number four is on the way. I'm rather worried the robes I have ordered for the festival won't fit.'

'Oh, congratulations, Nefi! I'm so pleased for you. Actually, I wanted to ask about the festival. What exactly is it?'

'The Festival of Tribute. What is it? It's a good excuse to eat and drink loads and loads, and wear new jewellery and the finest clothes, that's what it is. Not to mention all the presents we'll get. For Aki, it's an opportunity to show that he's the greatest Pharaoh there ever was. After all, he has the prettiest Queen ever, a brand new city and a shiny new religion. Aki will be giving what we call "The breath of life" to the visitors. In other words, do what I say, or you won't be breathing for much longer! Dignitaries from all over the world will come to prostrate themselves at his feet. Well, maybe not all over the world - where did you say you were from?'

'England.'

'No, still means nothing to me. Let's say, all over the civilised world.' Lucy couldn't protest; after all, she wasn't even sure if Britain had reached the iron age yet. She certainly preferred life in this sunny palace with its beautiful gardens and decorative lake to scrabbling around in the mist and the mud with a load of folk with blue faces. England could wait!

***

It was 1922, a week after Lucy had left Amarna, and Mary Chubb was cataloguing artefacts, getting a list ready for Division Day, the day when the Cairo museum would decide which of their treasures would stay in Egypt and which the archaeologists could take back to England. John entered the room holding the pot that the team had found in Nebkef's house on Lucy's last day.

'You've got a funny expression on your face,' said Mary.

'It's the strangest thing. I've been translating the hieroglyphics written on the base of this pot, and I've never seen anything like it before. Do you see this section here? A lion, the bird, a basket and two reeds. Well, that spells 'Lucy'. I've never, ever come across a 'Lucy' in ancient Egypt.'

'What does the rest of it say?'

It says, here in Regnal Year Five, I, Lucy, am honoured to serve Queen Nefertiti. Life, Prosperity, Health.'

'What a pity our Lucy isn't still here to see this,' replied Mary. 'I know! I'm going to telephone the hotel where she is staying. I'm sure she will be really pleased to hear of our discovery. Just fancy, another Lucy lived in Amarna two thousand years ago.'

***

After the initial elation at getting Big Bessie working properly again, Archie's mood had dropped to rock bottom. Any record of where and when Robert, James and Lucy had disappeared to was lost forever. His first port of call was the day that he had left Luxor in 1922. He enquired casually at the reception desk of the Winter Palace Hotel if anyone had seen the the three Baxters, but no luck. He paid a visit to the hotel each day for a week, but there was still no sign of them. After a brief conversation with Howard Carter's assistant to check all was well with their dig and that he wasn't needed in the Valley of the Kings, Archie tried the hotel one last time.

'Mr Baxter, Sir,' called the concierge, 'Telephone call for you.'

***

It was day eight in the second month of the planting season, and Lucy had an excellent view of The Festival of Tribute. It began with the arrival of Akhenaten and Nefertiti in a carrying chair. Nefertiti, her arm around her husband's waist, was clearly loving the occasion. Lucy wanted to jump up and down and wave and shout 'Woo hoo!' but she knew she had to do the same as everyone else and bow down meekly before the royal couple. Akhenaten and Nefertiti's two eldest daughters, Meri and Meket, walked behind their parents. Their other daughter, Ankhes, sat next to Lucy with her nurse, the Menat. Servants carried Akhenaten and Nefertiti to a stage, and they took their places on thrones shaded by a gilded, decorative, wooden canopy. Then followed the parade of all parades! One after another, men from all over the 'civilised' world, mostly countries that Egypt had subjugated, arrived bearing gifts. When the people from Africa appeared, Ankhes squealed in delight to see some walking with tame leopards on leashes. Others came from the Middle East and the Mediterranean, from countries Lucy couldn't have placed on a map, like Canaan and the Kingdom of Kheta. Lucy guessed that those countries probably had different names in her time. All the gifts were piled up around Akhenaten and Nefertiti: food, wine, weapons, vases and vast amounts of gold and silver. Lucy gasped in shock to see lines of men, roped together, shuffling along to join the offerings. Slaves!

Musicians and dancers performed in front of the stage. Acrobats, wrestlers and boxers put on a breathtaking show. It was such a colourful scene. Lucy was reminded of pop festivals, like Glastonbury, that she had seen on television. She was a long way from a festival site in Somerset, though, and unless Robert and James had managed to talk their way into The Festival of Tribute, she was sure that she was the only English person watching the spectacle. Or was she?

Lucy peered intently at a man struggling to get to his feet after stretching out on the ground before Akhenaten and Nefertiti. The Pharaoh and his Queen were chatting and didn't pay him any attention, but Lucy noticed every detail: the way he walked, his out-of-condition body, and how misshapen his robes were. Actually, even the red cross on a white background that decorated his cloak was a giveaway. Lucy made an excuse to the Menat and moved to get a closer look.

Through the laughter and cheering, the music and singing, one voice reached that strange foreign visitor.

'Uncle Archie! Uncle Archie! Uncle Archie!'

With all the excitement in the square, there was only one person who took any notice of the brief conversation between Lucy and Archie, and that was the servant, Omari. He was annoyed that he couldn't get close enough to hear what they were saying, as he was busy arranging the gifts on the platform. He had taken the gift that the man in the red and white cloak had brought, some kind of perfume, and had noticed something unusual about him. Omari knew only too well his own lowly place in society and saw that this man also lacked the air of self-importance that the other ambassadors exhibited. So, why would this strange foreign man be talking to the girl, the foreign friend of the Queen?

'Senebi,' he called to one of the other servants. 'Be witness to those two talking over there.'

'I see them. Why?'

'I don't know yet. Just bear witness to the fact that they seem to know each other.'

Lucy felt ecstatic as she returned to her place to watch the rest of the festival celebrations. Her plan had worked. The archaeologists working at the Amarna dig had found her message, written in hieroglyphics on the pot that she had buried, and had passed its curious content to her uncle. The decoration on the pot had provided a clue to the date,

'The first month of the planting season,' and also told of the glory of The Festival of Tribute that would follow. So, even though it was over two thousand years in the past, after a few trial runs, Archie had been able to find her. She chuckled when she thought about the present that her uncle had brought. He came bearing a gift of some awful aftershave that an aunt had given him two Christmases ago. It was still wrapped up in snowman wrapping paper - not a common sight in Egypt! Archie told Lucy that, although he couldn't be absolutely certain, he hoped he had set up Big Bessie to collect her at eight o'clock from the boundary stela where she had waited once before. Lucy had explained that Robert and James were in Karnak, so Archie said he would slip away shortly and return to the lab. Then he would go and find them.

Archie would have loved to have stayed longer to witness the spectacle, but he knew he wouldn't be able to relax until he had tracked down Robert and James. It wasn't as though anyone would notice his absence from the celebrations. In that, Archie was quite wrong. Omari was still on duty, but he had managed to have a quick word with a distant relative who was a guard. He, in turn, had spoken to his commanding officer, and now the news of Archie's presence had reached the ears of the Vizier, Nakht, who was in a meeting with the Pharaoh's advisor, Seti. Would Archie have felt honoured to be the subject of discussion by two of the most powerful people in Egypt? No, he would quite rightly have felt very worried.

'He's leaving.' said Nakht

'That proves it,' replied Seti,' If he were a genuine ambassador, he would not dishonour the Pharaoh by leaving early. He must be a spy.'

'Shall we kill him now?' asked Nakht.

'No, we must not draw attention to ourselves. We do not want to give visitors from other countries the idea that anyone might rise against mighty Egypt. Instead, we will follow him. He may lead us to more spies.'

Two hours later, six palace guards were crouched behind a rock, keeping an eye on the place where they had last seen the foreigner. They had expected him to head straight for the river, but instead, he had turned off and climbed the path that led to the first boundary stela. They watched as he sat down in the dark shadow where the statues of Akhenaten and Nefertiti were carved into the cliff face. There was no way out from there. They figured he must be waiting to meet someone, another spy perhaps. Six more men were sent to guard the route from the river. Now, it was just a waiting game!

Nakht was getting impatient.

'Have you heard anything yet? I'm missing the feast!'

'No, Sir. They are watching the boundary stela. No one will get past them.'

'I can't wait any longer. Arrest him and arrest the girl. If I don't join the feast soon, my presence will be missed.'

'Is it the Pharaoh calling you or your belly?' muttered the soldier as he walked back to give the message to the men who were keeping Archie under surveillance.

Another group of soldiers was at the entrance to the women's section of the Royal Palace. If they needed to, they would go in, but for the moment one of them was questioning the nurse .

'She's not here, I tell you. She came back with me because the children were tired. She helped me put them to bed. They've had quite enough excitement for one day. Then she went off somewhere, I don't know where. Have you tried the feast?' The soldier nodded. He was unsure what to do but knew he would get into trouble if he hadn't searched everywhere. He asked the Menat if she would show him around. He didn't know what all the fuss was about, but he needed to be thorough, so he spent an enjoyable hour exploring areas of the palace he would never usually be able to see with a woman that reminded him of his mum. The Menat, too, was enjoying the company of this young man, so she made sure he took his time and gave him plenty of fruit to keep him sustained. He reminded her of her own son, now long since grown up.

'Well?' demanded Nakht.

'It's not good news, Sir. When the soldiers stormed the position, he wasn't there. They swore he couldn't have slipped past them, even though it is dark now.'

'And the girl?'

'She can't be found either, Sir. We know she went to the palace with the nurse, but we don't know where she went after that.'

'She must be somewhere!' exploded Nakht. 'Search for her!'

Lucy was somewhere. She was back in her favourite place, at her artist's desk. Lucy read through the papyrus scroll she had just prepared. At the top, she had drawn a picture in the 'new' style, showing Nefertiti sitting alongside her three children, the 'bump' of her fourth clearly visible through her long white gown. The sun god Aten was high in the sky and at the tips of the sun's rays, as usual, were Aten's hands. Traditionally, the hands would only touch the Pharaoh, but he wasn't in this picture, so instead they rested on Nefertiti's shoulders. Lucy wrote the words' Life Prosperity, Health' beneath the image, after which she wrote:

'Dearest Nefi, I thought you looked radiant today. If

ever there was a woman destined to be a great ruler, it has to be you. Forgive me for writing to you, rather than speaking in person, but I did not want any negative news to come your way on this glorious day...' Lucy then explained that she needed to go back to England with her countryman and thanked Nefi for her friendship and for the comforts she had bestowed. Lucy left the scroll, together with a note asking for it to be given to the Queen, on the table of a man who would be meeting Nefertiti very shortly. He was a sculptor called Thutmose who had been commissioned to make Nefertiti's likeness. Lucy blew out her candle and left.

Lucy had plenty of time to walk to the boundary stela. As she set out on her way, she was aware of a commotion ahead of her. Dozens of soldiers were pouring out onto the street. They were splitting into groups to knock on the doors of houses along the way. Lucy shrank back into the shadows. She had no idea what they wanted, but she did not dare risk getting delayed. Instead, she crept quickly along one of the side roads that fanned away from the main route. She could see soldiers in this road too, first behind her, and then two more walking towards her. Lucy lay flat on top of a low wall and then slid off it to land on the other side. The men were so close now that she could hear their voices.

'So who is this foreign girl we've been sent to find?'

'I dunno. Someone that the Queen has befriended. We'll know her when we see her because she looks different from us. She's all pale, and her hair is the wrong colour...' Lucy reacted in two ways to this snippet of conversation On the one hand she was irritated: 'Cheek! I think my skin has turned a lovely colour in the sun, and as for my hair...' and on the other hand, she was thinking,

'Oh my goodness, they are trying to find me. That can't be good.'

As soon as the soldiers had passed by, Lucy was on the move. Whilst her sense of direction wasn't great, (Robert's was much better) her logical mind guided her. To start with, she knew that she needed to be following paths that led uphill. It wasn't going to be the quickest way, but Lucy knew that eventually, she would reach the cliffs that encircled the city. Then all she had to do was keep them on her right, and eventually, she would arrive at the first boundary stela. Lucy passed several other stelae on the way, but there was no time to pause for sightseeing. It was a long, rocky and challenging path and several times she stumbled in the dark, grazing her knees. Lucy had a growing sense of dread because she had no idea what time it was. She had started out with plenty of time to spare. Now she was probably late.

It seemed an age. Travelling around a city takes so much longer than walking through the centre, but at last she saw them, the two towering sculptures standing in a recess, next to hieroglyphics carved into the cliffside. She started to run. She might be too late! Rocks at her feet scattered and tumbled down the path. Then there was a shout:

'There she is!' Six bored soldiers who had spent all day watching this position jumped up. Lucy hadn't expected anyone to be lying in wait and they hadn't expected anyone to come from her direction. Lucy did the only thing she could and ran as fast as her aching legs would carry her. She reached the monument and clutched at the base of the Queen's sculpture.

'Help me Nefi,' she panted.

CHAPTER EIGHTEEN

Robert and James returned to the palace at Karnak. It had taken them a long time to get back as they had had to hitch a ride on several boats. Usually, they only saw priests in the temple, but walking ahead of them now was a burly soldier. He didn't appear to be the most pleasant of characters; the boys saw him give a violent shove to one of the doorkeepers who didn't get out of his way quickly enough. The poor man went sprawling on the ground

'Charming,' said James, as he helped the doorkeeper to his feet. 'Who's that?'

'That's General Potasimto. He's come to see Asim.'

'I'll tell you what,' whispered Robert to James, as they continued on their way, 'I'm going to run on ahead and eavesdrop. You never know, Maya might need our help.'

'Be careful, Robert. Stay out of the way of Potato-head.'

Robert slipped into Asim's room behind Potasimto, only to find that Maya was already inside.

'Hail to you, High Priest Maya, may the god Amun always favour your house,' said Potasimto.

'There has to be no record of our meeting. We are in a difficult situation, facing peril from all sides, and we look to you to assist us and serve Amun. There is danger ahead.'

'I have no fear,' replied Potasimto haughtily.

'We think an individual has been sent here from the underworld by the serpent god Apophis. Ever since he arrived, the fortunes of this temple have been sliding away. He has to be stopped. He must be returned to that place of torment, to hell.'

'I will smite him with my club,' roared Potasimto,

'Shhhh,' urged Asim.

'I will smite him with my club,' whispered Potasimto. Robert couldn't see if Potato Head had brought a club with him, but he didn't doubt that smiting would be at the top of his list if he got his hands on one. He wondered who they were talking about.

'Where do I find this snake, and how will I know him?' growled Potasimto. Robert's blood ran cold when he heard Maya's reply.

'My spies have sent word. He has arrived back in Thebes and is on his way back from the Nile. He has red hair, and he calls himself James.'

Robert ran at full pelt to find James.

'Change of plan.' he gasped, 'You can't go to meet Asim; it's Potato-head. He's a contract killer, and it's you he's after.'

'Crikey! Let's head for the Nile'

'No, you hide in the inner temple, where we first arrived, and I'll investigate.'

Twenty minutes later, Robert returned.

'It's no good, James. Potato-head seems to have brought the rest of his army with him. There are soldiers everywhere. You can't get in or out of the palace. What's worse, remember that doorkeeper that we saw Potato-head knock over? He's just dangled him upside down and threatened him until he admitted that he had seen us in the palace.' Just then, the boys heard someone clap their hands three times, and the large double doors of the inner temple began to swing open. In the distance a gong rang out and a long line of priests filed into the room. It was time for the ceremony the twins had witnessed when they had first arrived in Ancient Egypt, 'The Drawing of the Bolt'. James' initial fear subsided when he realised that the priests weren't paying him any attention. They were used to seeing him around, and they obviously were not part of the plot. James moved well away from the altar so that the priests could pile up the offerings for the god, Amun. It was a precious time for the priests because they feared that the Pharaoh would soon ban all ceremonies not dedicated to Aten soon.

Unfortunately, Robert and James did not see Maya enter the room, spot James, and quietly leave again. However, they couldn't fail to notice the huge frame of Potato-head as he strode in and let out a great roar, the kind of noise intended to chill the blood of his enemies. Strangely, it had the effect of shocking James into action. They say a drowning man sees his life flash before his eyes. In James' case, what came to mind was the last tutorial with his drama teacher, who had criticised his underwhelming performance. He realised he could never win a physical fight with this beast of a man; he needed to play to his own strengths. Not caring if anyone overheard him, he called to Robert:

'It's time they knew I am a god. Help me.' Then he turned to address those in the room, most of whom were staring at Potato-head. 'Behold. I am the god 'Ferarri' the patron of all things red.' James stretched his arms out wide. Robert grabbed him around the waist and lifted him a few inches off the ground so that, to those watching, it looked like he was hovering unaided. The priests gasped, but one man kept moving steadily forward - Potato-head.

'In the name of the god Eff-one, I command you to stop!' shouted James. The General didn't show any signs of stopping. Robert was alarmed to see that he now seemed to have been reunited with his club. It was an unsophisticated weapon, consisting of a ball of stone mounted on a wooden shaft, but it looked deadly. Robert lowered James back to the ground; he needed a weapon too. Robert turned and picked up… a pomegranate.

'Carry on,' he hissed to James, then turned towards Potato-head. Robert was good at most sports and one he excelled at was cricket. He tossed the pomegranate from hand to hand, took aim and threw. The priests wailed in surprise as the pomegranate appeared to dance before them, then hurtle through the air and smack Potato-head right between the eyes. He grunted and stepped back. Then came another pomegranate, and another.

'Behold the power of Ferarri,' shouted James. Whilst the priests in the room were now on their knees, bowing down before James, the General was enraged. He wasn't going to be beaten by fruit! Robert had run out of pomegranates. A watermelon headed in Potato-head's direction, but although it looked dramatic flying through the air, he batted it away easily with his club. He was almost upon James now. He lifted the club high up in the air. In a moment, he would bring it down with full force on James' head. Robert rushed behind Potato-head and, just as he lifted the club above his own head to achieve more backswing, Robert jumped up, grabbed the weapon and pulled hard. Potato-head was so surprised that he overbalanced and fell backwards. Robert hadn't expected his manoeuvre to be so successful and he let go of the club to get out of Potato-head's way. James saw what happened next. The club went sailing through the air and hit a ceramic statue of Amun, shattering it to pieces.

After the last fragment fell to the floor, there was a moment's silence. Then a voice rang out. It was the young doorkeeper Potato-head had bullied earlier.

'Sacrilege! He has dishonoured Amun!' As Potato-head tried to struggle to his feet, he found himself overpowered by priests flinging themselves on top of him. Maybe he could have defeated ten priests, but not fifty or sixty of them. He disappeared beneath a seething mass of white robes.

Just when James and Robert were thinking that the occasion couldn't have gone any better, they heard the grunt and groan of someone trying to keep their feet after landing on the altar amidst a pile of fruit.

'Uncle Archie!' gasped James.

'Hello boys, I'm only here for two minutes; I just thought I would take a quick look to check if I had set the coordinates right. You seem to have your hands full!'

'Can we come back with you now?' asked Robert.

'I haven't set your coordinates yet, but I will as soon as I get back. Just climb up here, and two minutes after I have gone, it will be your turn. Can you improvise for a bit?

You seem to have the situation under control.'

'No probs!' replied James with a grin. 'I'm hoping I will get nominated for an Oscar.'

The room was hushed. The priests had watched the young god, Ferarri, talking in a strange language to an old man who had appeared from nowhere. Now, the red-headed boy turned towards them. Those nearest to him thought they heard someone whisper:

'Maya is at the back of the room.'

'Behold, you see behind me an envoy from Amun,' said James. Now was the time to name-drop because Amun was clearly the big cheese around here. James rather spoiled the majesty of his speech by adding, 'We're best mates!' But then he picked up the tone again: 'Amun decrees that from this day forth, the only way to undo the harm you have done is to change from the top down. You!' James pointed at Maya. 'You will relinquish the High Priesthood and return to work on your family's farm, and this temple will now be in the good hands of …You!' James pointed at the young doorkeeper, who gasped and fell to his knees. To emphasise the point, Archie also pointed theatrically at the boy and then, amazing everyone, promptly disappeared. Big Bessie had called.

Robert climbed onto the altar platform and hauled James up after him to continue his speech from aloft. It was yet another supernatural action that reinforced James' god-like status. He didn't worry about his audience now. James knew he had them in the palm of his hand. Potato-head had stopped struggling and Maya was prostrate on the floor. For Maya and the General, it was one thing thinking James was a demon from the underworld, but now that they knew he was a friend of Amun's…

'The punishment for General Potato whatsisname is

to be thrown in the Nile, naked, in front of all his men, and any soldiers that don't laugh are to be tossed in the water too. Tonight, you shall all have a party, with the best food and drink, music and dancing to celebrate the day when Ferarri was on the podium.' James was wondering how he could explain that they had to grow tomatoes so that they could make pizzas when Big Bessie stepped in, and the scene vanished.

'I was just getting going,' said James, as he and Robert came out from behind the screen in Uncle Archie's lab. 'Nice to be wearing jeans again though. I presume you've ditched your skirt, Robert.'

'Sure have; these feel like my favourite sports shorts. Hello, Uncle Archie. Your timing was excellent.'

'Where's Lucy,' asked James, 'Do we have to go and rescue her?'

'I was hoping that she would be here by now. I had to leave her to her own resources while I came to look for you.'

As if in answer to him, the lights flickered in the room, and there was Lucy.

'Thank you, Nefi,' she murmured.

'I think you will find her name is Big Bessie,' announced James. 'Good, now we are all together, let's have a cup of tea.'

***

'So what happened to Big Bessie, Uncle?' asked Lucy.

'Firstly, there was a leak which caused her to malfunction and that sent you to Ancient Egypt. Right place, wrong time. I had to rewrite a lot of the code and I have to admit I made a few mistakes. I was working under pressure and too quickly. I typed a minus instead of a plus in the code for a male. So it meant that you, Lucy, stayed

177

put, but the boys jumped around in time a bit.'

'We've been away a long time, and we know being invisible isn't good for you, Robert. Uncle, do we know how long Robert has got before he starts feeling ill.' asked Lucy.

'It's still a mystery, I'm afraid.'

'But are we any further forward?' she pressed. 'Has Big Bessie given us any more clues? All we had is 'Tut', and he wasn't even born when we were in Ancient Egypt and, in 1922, we left before they had found him.'

'Well, I do have something, but I don't know what it means. As usual, Big Bessie is being somewhat cryptic, but she gave us this clue: 'A shave before the sun goes down: call the servant from the tomb.'

'What can it mean?' asked Lucy. 'Does she want some kind of razor?'

'It's a long time since my face had any contact with a razor,' chuckled Archie.

'I didn't see anybody shaving in Egypt,' said Lucy, worriedly.

'Nor did we, although most people were close-shaven, except for the Pharaoh - he wore a daft false beard,' said James

'Maybe we are going down the wrong track,' said Lucy. 'Why is the servant in a tomb? Wait a moment! In the artist's studio, I made some little figurines; shabtis. They represented servants who would do all the work in the afterlife for whoever was buried in the tomb.'

'Shabti?' said Robert. 'I've never heard of a shabti.' Archie typed into his laptop.

'Here, they look like these.'

'Oh, a dolly!' We had one of those,' said James proudly. 'We buried it.' James and Robert then briefly told

Archie and Lucy about how the Nubian girl in Aswan had given them the shabti.

'What if Big Bessie wants one of the ones I made?' wondered Lucy. 'Where did you bury yours, James, and what's the connection with shaving?' Robert told them how he had buried it at the point of a shadow cast by a pyramid.

'What time was it when you buried it?' asked Archie excitedly.

'Not sure. All I know is we thought it would be dark in an hour or so.'

'I don't suppose you know what month it was?'

'No, the names of their months were different from ours. It was about a week before the floods, and it was the same year you found us.' Archie typed furiously into his laptop while the others waited patiently.

'Aha!' he exclaimed. 'There's an expression that I wouldn't expect you to know. Robert describing where he buried the shabti made me think of it. "Five o'clock shadow." It means that if you have had a shave in the morning, your chin is getting a little dark by five o'clock. You see, we know it was just before the flood season because you said the priest was expecting farmers to come and paint the Sphinx; therefore we can say that it must have been June, and I've just looked up when the sun went down in that month. So you will have been burying your Shabti at five o'clock.'

'I'll nip back and get it,' said Robert. 'It had better be me because no one can see me. What year shall I go?'

'I'm pretty sure it won't be there now,' replied Archie, 'Someone will have discovered it. So perhaps you should go, say, in the 1600s. A century after that, you might bump into Napoleon; they say his troops blew the nose off the Sphinx while using it for target practice. In the 1800s, people started to get interested in Egyptian archaeology, so they might have found it if it was there then. Start in 1600, and if it's not there then, we'll try earlier.'

Archie, James and Lucy waited apprehensively, nursing cold cups of tea. Then, at last, the lab lights flickered, Big Bessie hummed, and they heard a cry from behind the screen.

'Got it! It was buried under quite a lot of sand.' Robert placed the shabti on the table. Gradually it materialised. James couldn't resist saying:

'Hello Dolly,' and then, while his uncle placed the shabti under Big Bessie's scanner, he proceeded to entertain the others with a very passable version of Louis Armstrong's hit song from the musical, "Hello Dolly." Big Bessie whirred into life. Lucy clutched Robert's invisible hand. A bell sounded, and a notification flashed on the monitor:

'Stage one scan completed; exhibit added to museum catalogue. Enter Stage 2.'

Unfortunately, Robert was still invisible.

Archie read out the rest of the clue. It was the word 'Oxford' followed by two sets of numbers.

'But we're in Cambridge, not Oxford,' complained Robert. Lucy was thoughtful.

'Oxford is not just famous for its University,' she said, 'It's also the name of a Dictionary.'

'Of course!', said Archie, 'It will be the date of the edition, and hopefully the page number. I'll sort this one out. I haven't got that edition, but I can go and buy one. I've only got to go back a year. I'll quickly reset Big Bessie. Why don't you put the kettle on and look for some more biscuits?'

***

Archie leafed through the dictionary. His trip back in time had been uneventful and now, as they all gathered around him, he paused on the page in question.

'Look what is at the top of the page,' exclaimed Lucy, and she read: "A piece of jewellery in the shape of a large flat coin worn on a chain around the neck." It's the definition of a medallion. We were all given one in Luxor.'

'Ah!' sighed Archie, 'Another tale to tell you about. I was briefly in Aswan, got arrested and last saw it on a table in an Egyptian military prison.'

'No, no, no!' exclaimed James, 'We found it, in Nubia, by the Ramses Temple, only it was underwater, didn't we Robert? So we've got all four.'

'Ohhh!' It was Robert's turn to sigh, 'I haven't told you about this. You won't know, because you can't see me, but I'm not wearing them. Something happened. I don't know if it was a dream, or a fever from when I was ill after an infection from a mosquito bite, but James, you know when we got 'blipped' and ended up in the tomb with the grave robbers? Well, it wasn't the first time I had been in Tutankhamun's tomb.' Robert then told the others about his adventures during that strange and disturbing night.

'Had you any idea what you were going to find in the tomb? Did you do any research before you went?' asked Archie. James and Lucy immediately burst out laughing.

'Research?' giggled Lucy, 'It's Robert you're talking to. If it doesn't involve tactics, or a team, or a scoreline, then research doesn't interest Robert.' Her brother joined in with the laughter; he knew it was true! Archie quizzed him some more on things he had seen when the grave robbers captured James, especially on the contents of the sealed rooms.

'There's no doubt about it.' said Archie solemnly.

'Harry Burton took thousands of photographs of Howard Carter's discovery. If you haven't researched this, then you can only know by having been there. You have described things I recognise from those photographs. The jars for the entrails you described, they call them canopic jars. They are in the Egyptian Museum in Cairo now, but they are not wearing our medallions! Our time in Egypt isn't finished yet. We are going to have to go back to 1922 and find them before anyone else does!'

'Oh, good. Does that mean we're going back to the Winter Palace Hotel? There were a few things on the menu I haven't tried yet,' said James.

'First thing I want is a soak in the bath, said Lucy, 'And I wouldn't mind some modern cosmetics. I've been using soap made from clay and oil, and moisturiser made from milk and honey, not to mention using burnt almonds as eyeliner.'

'Soap!' mused Robert, 'Remind me what that is again!'

CHAPTER NINETEEN

Friday, 24 November 1922

'Herbie!' cried Archie. Lord Carnarvon was accompanied by a young lady wearing a large floppy hat when they arrived by donkey in the Valley of the Kings. There wasn't a road or a decent path from the river, so this was the best way to travel, but Archie felt that Lord Carnarvon looked very incongruous seated on a donkey. He was a man who was more used to the world of racehorses and fast cars.

'Archie, my good man, meet my daughter, Evelyn.' Archie had researched what would be happening in the next few days, and he knew that twenty-one-year-old Evelyn would be present when the tomb was opened.

'Howard Carter has been like a cat on a hot tin roof

waiting for your arrival,' said Archie. Herbie laughed.

'Now there's an expression I've never heard before. "Cat on hot bricks", I know, but a tin roof! Who has a tin roof anyway?'

'Note to self,' thought Archie as he guided his visitors to the tomb, 'Think before you speak. It's no good using American expressions to a very English lord!' Archie waved at Lucy and James, who were watching from a distance, and they waved back. 'My nephew and niece,' he explained. Of course, he didn't point out that his other nephew, Robert, would be following their every move once they were inside the tomb.

From the reports that Howard Carter had sent him three weeks earlier, Lord Carnarvon already knew that the team had found a doorway to a new tomb, and that Carter could see from the broken seal that someone had gained entry in the distant past; the tomb had evidently been resealed in antiquity. Most importantly, the seal was that of the boy king, Tutankhamun. There was plenty of activity now as men carried away baskets full of the rubble that had been blocking the stairway. Now that Lord Carnarvon had inspected the outer doorway, the team could move on to the next stage.

'Is that it for today?' asked Robert.

'Yes, it's a slow business this archaeology game. No need for you three to come back for a couple of days.'

Sunday, 26 November 1922

Lord Carnarvon and Evelyn had walked down the sloping tunnel, now cleared of rubble, and were watching Howard Carter prising out stones from the sealed doorway to the tomb itself. A little way further back sat Robert; this tunnel was getting to be like a second home to him now.

When the hole was big enough, Howard Carter thrust his arm through and, by the light of a candle, peered into the space beyond. There was silence. Robert knew what Howard could see, but no one else did. Eventually, Lord Carnarvon could bear the suspense no longer.

'Can you see anything?'

'Yes, wonderful things!' breathed Howard Carter.

Officially, that was as far as the discovery was supposed to go. The archaeologists had to wait another day for a visit by an official from the Egyptian Department of Antiquities. Robert retreated up the tunnel to allow the party to leave, then quickly nipped back inside as they passed him. At first, he was alone, and then he wasn't because Howard's assistant, Arthur 'Pecky' Callender, arrived to rig up electric lighting ready for tomorrow's visit. Robert left the tomb again and went to where Uncle Archie was waiting. He wasn't the only one outside because, much to Howard Carter's annoyance, news of the discovery had spread far and wide, and from this moment on, he was to be plagued by hordes of sightseers.

James and Lucy had returned to the hotel and were enjoying fine dining, but Robert was delighted to find that Archie had brought a picnic and eagerly explored the hamper. At last Pecky Callender started to pack up. A wooden grille had been fitted as a temporary door over the entrance to the tomb, and Robert was able to slip behind it before it was closed and locked. He had brought along a snack from the picnic basket so as to be prepared in case it was a long night before he could get out of the tomb again. Pecky had switched off the lights, but Robert had thought ahead and brought candles with him, and he lit one now. He made his way back easily to the blocked-up doorway. The hole made by Howard Carter was big enough for him to wriggle through. He knew he need not look in the first storeroom, the antechamber, where there were hundreds of objects that would keep Howard Carter busy for years; Robert needed to find his way through to the Burial Chamber.

Another sealed doorway presented an obstacle. It was blocked with mud bricks, and Robert knew that he had to create an opening in it to get to where the canopic jars were stored. If the tomb had been in pristine condition, he might have had a problem, but it was evident from the items strewn about on the floor that grave robbers had visited in the past, so he could blame them for any mess he made. They had lived thousands of years ago; they were hardly going to complain!

Eventually, Robert was able to wriggle through the hole he had made and enter the Burial Chamber. He lit another candle and the flame illuminated the vast gold shrine that almost filled the space. From here, it was straightforward; he edged his way to the small room that Uncle Archie had told him was called the treasury. He gave a little start when his candlelight caught two eyes staring back at him, before he remembered the black sculpture seated on a chest that he had seen on his previous visit. It was the god Anubis guarding the necropolis in the form of a jackal atop his shrine.

Robert had to use all his strength to remove the lid of the alabaster canopic casket. He was terrified that he might drop it and cause it to crack or even shatter. Locating them by touch, Robert felt the heads inside the casket. He realised that they weren't stoppers to jars; the whole casket had been carved with four internal compartments. He wondered if he dared look inside one but then thought that three-thousand-year-old intestines could wait a while longer before being discovered. He quickly retrieved the medallions from where Tut had placed them and hung them around his neck, tucking them inside his shirt so they would not get caught when he scrambled through the narrow doorways. In the half-light, before they turned invisible, the medallions looked a little different from how he remembered them.

It was time to retrace his steps. With a great effort Robert raised the casket lid and put it back in place. He repaired the hole he had created as tidily as possible and made his way to the antechamber doorway. He noticed a candle flickering on the other side of the entrance hole and quickly blew out the one he was carrying. He knew he hadn't left a candle alight, so who had? Suddenly, all was dark. Someone was wriggling through the hole. Robert stepped aside as the small figure of Lady Evelyn Leonora Almina Herbert landed in a heap on the tomb floor.

'Oh, I say! What a wheeze!' she exclaimed.

'This isn't in the history books,' thought Robert as Howard Carter and Lord Carnarvon followed. 'So, they are making a secret night-time visit to the tomb.' Robert then climbed through the hole. There was so much excitement behind him in the antechamber that no one noticed what little sound he made. Howard's assistant, Pecky, was on the other side of the doorway. He was too large to fit through the hole! Then it was onwards, up through the tunnel and out into the night, where Robert was reunited with his Uncle.

'Got them!' he said, smiling and patting his chest, making the medallions jingle.

CHAPTER TWENTY

After collecting Lucy and James from the hotel, the Baxters continued their journey back to the twenty-first century. Soon all four were sitting around the table in the lab.

'Okay, Robert,' said James, 'Let's see them then.'

'They're already on the table; you'll see them in a moment.'

'Goodness!' gasped Lucy as they materialised. 'Are you sure these are them? They've changed!'

'Quite sure, they've been around my neck since I found them in the canopic chest.' Lying on the table, glinting in the light, were four discs made from faience - a blue glazed ceramic popular in Ancient Egypt. Lucy picked one of them up; on one side was engraved the image of the sun god, Aten, on the other side were hieroglyphics.

'I've got a good feeling about this,' said James. 'Surely, this is going to do the trick.' Archie placed the medallions under the scanner and pressed the start button. Big Bessie hummed and purred, and the Baxters heard the 'ping' that came when she registered an item into the museum catalogue.

'Hooray!' shouted James, 'I knew it.'

'Err, guys,' came a voice from behind the table. They turned their heads, but they couldn't see anyone. Robert was still invisible.

'Oh, that's a drag. What's the monitor displaying?'

'It says "House of Rebirth: an extra go." What can that mean?' wondered Archie.

'I know, I know, I know!' cried James excitedly. 'It's from a board game called senet. We played it with Tut. He gave us a travelling set. It all links up. Do you remember, Robert, we used to play it on the rooftop where we slept.'

'Where is it now?' asked Lucy.

'I don't know about now,' replied Robert, 'But three thousand years ago, it was still on the rooftop. I hid it in a corner under our reed mats.'

'Then we have to get it,' said James. 'I'll go because if it's gone missing, I'll be able to ask someone if they've seen it.'

'Do we know when he should arrive?' asked Lucy.

'We certainly do,' replied Archie. 'I know there was a period when you were lost out in the wilderness, but once I had located you, Big Bessie was able to keep track. As you know, the essential rule in space-time exploration is that you must have no face-to-face contact with yourself. I'm not sure what would happen if you did. I just know it wouldn't be good! So, anyway, I can set the coordinates for you to go back to Egypt on the same day you were in Karnak doing your god Ferrari act. I can't set you down in the temple, of course, but with a bit of guesswork I can get you somewhere near where you stayed. That way there will be no danger of you meeting yourself.'

Big Bessie set James down on a rooftop. Fortunately, it was a flat rooftop like all the houses in this district of Thebes, but, unfortunately, it was the wrong one. James studied the neighbouring houses and was confident he could identify where he needed to be. From his vantage point, he could also see that the house whose roof he was standing on was built around a central courtyard and he could hear music drifting up to him. He raced down the stairs, then paused for a moment.

'Cool,' he thought, 'A party. I'll run and get the senet set and then pop in.' He was in luck. The board game was still where Robert had hidden it and, with the incentive of having some entertainment before Big Bessie collected him, he ran back at a speed that would have impressed his brother. When he arrived back at the courtyard, he discovered the source of the music. A small group of musicians sat in a shady corner. Amongst them were men playing a flute and a lute, but the dominant rhythmic beat came from tambourines, cymbals and drums.

'Hello,' said James,' I hope you don't mind me watching.' He noticed a curious metal instrument lying on the ground. Encouraged by the smiling musicians he picked it up.' What's this called?'

'It's a sistrum.' James realised that he had seen musicians playing it in the temple's inner sanctum. It was in the shape of a small tennis racquet strung with metal rings. He shook it. What a great rattling noise it made! James listened for a moment. One, two, three, pause. One, two, three, pause. He picked up the beat and joined in.

'We are practising for the Opet festival,' shouted one of the musicians. 'It's a procession alongside the Nile.' Then, to James' delight, a group of dancers appeared. First came dark-skinned girls, Nubians, whose dance moves resembled modern-day gymnastics. They performed cartwheels and flips and bent over backwards to walk like a crab. Following them were two girls wearing striking costumes. Embroidery embellished their sleeves, which had been made to look like eagle wings. They performed an elaborate dance, wrapping their wings around themselves and each other. Then, in complete contrast, a group of men enacted battle scenes using long staves. It reminded James of martial arts. After that there was a lull, although the musicians kept playing. The next set of dancers wasn't ready.

One of the musicians caught James' eye and gestured to him to join in with the dancing. James didn't need a second invitation. He always gladly seized any opportunity to perform, but what kind of dance should he do? He could breakdance, but that didn't go with this music and he would need a partner for any kind of ballroom dance. Then in a flash of inspiration - a Jumping Jack Flash - he remembered a video of Mick Jagger onstage with the Rolling Stones in the 1960s, shaking a tambourine and gyrating around the stage. Then he thought about the time the Baxters had been stuck in 1966 and were watching the hippies dancing on a lawn near the river Thames. He flung down his sistrum and gave the Egyptians some no-holds-barred freestyle groovy moves involving lots of head-shaking, hip-wiggling and arm-waving. He grinned as he heard the enthusiastic shouts of his new band of brothers, the musicians.The next dancers were waiting to begin. He beckoned them forward, and they shyly joined in as he weaved through them to leave. It was hard to leave, but he didn't want to outstay his welcome and in any case, he had an appointment with Big Bessie. Waving goodbye, he grabbed the senet set and raced up to the roof.

Shortly afterwards, a curious dancer climbed the stairs, only to find the rooftop empty. Later, when she heard the tale of what had happened in the temple that day, of how Ferrari had defeated General Potasimto, all became clear. She had been dancing with a god.

***

'Got it!' cried James as he arrived back in the lab, 'Gordon Bennett, I've found the Senet!'

'Who was Gordon Bennett anyway? I know it's something people say,' wondered Robert.

'I'll look it up while Uncle Archie scans the senet set,' said Lucy, reaching for a laptop. A few minutes later, she had the answer. 'He was a playboy who owned the New York Herald at the end of the nineteenth century and he was famous for outrageous stunts. It's more of a British saying, really, used when faced with something unexpected.'

That was exactly the situation they found themselves in a few moments later when a shrill alarm bell rang in the lab. Lucy clapped her hands over her ears. Fortunately, the din only lasted for a few minutes. A warning message flashed up on Big Bessie's monitor.

'What's happening?' Lucy asked as she looked around the room for Robert. He was still invisible.

'Ah!' replied Archie, 'Big Bessie won't accept this board game into our catalogue because it's also on display in the Cairo Museum along with other exhibits from Tutankhamun's tomb.'

'So, what does that mean?' asked Robert.

'It means we have to put it back in the tomb where Howard Carter found it; Everything was photographed and labelled and, remember, we can't change history.'

'Shall I go back?' asked Robert?

'I think you may have to,' replied Archie, 'But you can't go back when you were there before because you would meet yourself, and then there is the problem of the secret visitors who went in after you.'

'I'm just reading about it now, Uncle,' called Lucy from behind the laptop. 'Hold on a moment. Why don't you put the kettle on?'

The Baxters were seated around the table five minutes later, sustained by tea and biscuits, listening to Lucy.

'I've been looking at a plan of the tomb. Howard Carter discovered a little room behind the one he called the antechamber, which he named the Annex, and they were in there.'

'I didn't even know there was a room there,' said Robert.

'Howard spotted it by looking under a couch. There was a tiny opening leading to it, probably cut by grave robbers. The floor level of the room is about three feet lower than the antechamber and the room was a complete mess, even worse than your room, James!'

'Cheek!'

'There was a reason. The thieves had been in there and ransacked the place looking for gold, silver and perfume.'

'Perfume?' quizzed Robert.

'Yes,' continued Lucy, 'Perfumes, oils and ointments were very valuable. Not only that, once the thieves had poured them out of the original containers, they couldn't be traced back to the tomb. Anyway, the point of the story is that, because the room was such a jumble, Howard Carter decided to leave it until last. There turned out to be more than two thousand items in there, so they didn't start clearing the room until October 1927. They finished in the Spring of 1928, so we can pick a date from within that time frame.'

***

Lucy was still researching on the laptop.

'What's all this about the curse of Tutankhamun,' she piped up. 'It's supposed to affect anyone who's been in the tomb. They die!'

'James and I have been in the tomb,' said Robert anxiously, 'Do we need to worry about it?'

'No, it's all rubbish, invented by the newspapers and fuelled by the imagination of the author, Sir Arthur Conan Doyle,' replied Archie. 'However, there is something that has been bothering me; I need to go back and say goodbye to Herbie.'

'Goodness!' Everyone turned to look at Lucy. 'It says here that Lord Carnarvon died less than a year after they discovered the tomb.'

'I know, but as I said, there was no curse. Herbie contracted pneumonia and blood poisoning after an infected mosquito bite. That's why I need to say goodbye to him. Herbie loved fast cars and racehorses - action sports - but he was actually very frail himself.'

'I'm reading about the curse now,' replied Lucy,' Howard Carter lived for another sixteen years, Evelyn lived for another fifty-seven years and the guard, Sergeant Richard Adamson, didn't die until 1982, so it doesn't look like you two need to worry.'

'A good man, the Sergeant, we got quite friendly in the short time I knew him,' said Archie.

Archie was only gone for five minutes, although he had been back in 1922 for the whole of an afternoon. Lucy spotted that his eyes were a bit reddened, and she rushed over to hug him.

'A difficult goodbye,' he said, 'There is nothing I can do to change anything. I've always known this day would come but I couldn't let on about what was going to happen.'

'It was the same for us with Tut,' said James. 'People were always wishing him Life, Prosperity and Health, but we knew he would die young.'

'Do we know what year we are going back to Egypt, Uncle? I'm pretty bushed; it's been a long day, and I'm ready for bed,' asked Lucy.

'I've decided the best date will be a few days before Howard Carter starts to clear the annex. When I popped back to see Herbie in 1922, I made the hotel reservation. It caused a bit of a stir because they hadn't started taking bookings for 1927 yet. It will only take me a moment to set up Big Bessie. We needn't go back up to Karnak; there's a little outhouse at the back of the Winter Palace Hotel, which will do us fine. So, you'll be tucked up in bed in a jiffy.'

***

James sang at the top of his voice:
'Were you ever in Quebec
Stowing cargo on the deck?
There's the king with a golden crown
Riding on a donkey.'

The Baxters were indeed riding donkeys as they slowly made their way through the Valley of the Kings. Robert didn't think it was fair on the donkey to double up with James or Lucy, so he trotted alongside. They weren't going

196

fast anyway, and he was glad of the exercise.

'Tutankhamun sings this tune
Didn't like his tiny room
So he's gone and left his tomb
Riding on a donkey.'

'Actually,' said Archie, 'After they had studied Tutankhamun's mummy, Howard Carter insisted that it should remain in the tomb, where it lies to this day. It's displayed in a glass case.

That's good,' said Lucy, 'It shows respect.'

'Oh, I could tell you some tales about mummies that were shown absolutely no respect.'

'Such as?' asked James.

'For instance, from the thirteenth to the seventeenth century, mummies were chopped up and given to people as medicine.'

'Oh yuck!' cried Lucy.

'Here's another. A nineteenth-century American paper-manufacturer called Stanwood imported mummies stolen by Bedouin tribesmen and used the linen wrappings to make brown paper. He only stopped after a cholera outbreak.'

'Gross!'

They passed a large group of Egyptian workers pushing carts along a lightweight railway track. Men picked up the track sections after each carriage had passed over them and ran to fix them in front. The carriages contained artefacts from the tomb and were on their way to the Nile, where they would be loaded onto barges for the two-day journey to the Cairo Museum, escorted by armed guards.

'Glad to see that seems to be working smoothly. My idea, you know,' said Archie proudly.

There was no mistaking where the entrance to the

tomb was because a crowd of tourists was waiting opposite it, hoping for a glimpse of Tutankhamun's treasures.

The Baxters dismounted, bunched together so that Robert was protected in the middle, and weaved their way to the front. The sightseers were standing behind a low wall, kept at bay by the presence of a British soldier on guard duty.

Archie stepped around the wall and stood at the top of the steps leading to the tomb which was now barred by a heavy iron gate. The children followed and Archie called out to the soldier, who was just about to come rushing over to force them back.

'Sarge! It's me, Archie. How are you?'

'Eeeh! Flipping heck, so it is,' said the soldier with a broad Yorkshire accent. 'Hot and dusty is how I am, and have been for the last five years.'

'James and Lucy, I would like to introduce you to Sergeant Richard Adamson,' said Archie, 'He's doing a valiant job guarding the tomb.'

'I came to Luxor to collect some Army surveying equipment back in '22, and somehow I never left! What brings you here, Archie?'

'I was hoping to take a peek in the tomb, and also hoping for a favour from my old pal,' said Archie, slapping the man on the back.

'Sorry, if it were up to me, I would, but you need permission from Mr Carter. He's working over in an empty tomb they use to carry out the restoration work on Tut's treasures. As far as I know, Pecky will be going down this one with Harry. Did you meet Harry Burton, the photographer?'

'No, he came just after I left. I hear he's very good.'

The Baxters found Howard Carter talking to two

assistants in the tomb of Seti II. He looked up and nodded in answer to Archie's greeting but it was hardly a warm welcome, more an expression of 'what now? I've got work to do.' Archie's heart sank. It didn't look like Howard Carter was going to let them inside Tutankhamun's tomb. Lucy couldn't contain herself any longer.

'Oh! that's wonderful!' She was looking at a small, gold, decorative box inlaid with faience. 'I would love to paint that. Will it go to the museum in Cairo?'

'Yes,' replied Howard Carter, 'One day you will get your chance to study it there, but we have work to do with it first.'

'I've heard that you are a really good painter.'

'Well, it's true, I did use to dabble a bit. Actually that's what got me interested in all this. Of course, now we have Harry Burton to photograph everything.'

'Oh yes, but comparing it with a painting, I don't think you can't express the beauty of these objects through a black and white photograph. I can see why it's so important to have an accurate record of this investigation, though. You are obviously very organised.'

'It all takes time,' replied Howard Carter.

'But so worth it!'

'Well, young lady,' said Howard Carter, 'Would you like to see Harry Burton at work? He's going down into Tutankhamun's tomb shortly.'

'Thank you, that would be wonderful! Can I bring my uncle and brother?'

'And do you like Egyptology too?' Carter asked James.

'Oh, yes!' said James earnestly, perhaps a bit too earnestly, 'I especially like scenes of the Pharaohs hunting from chariots.'

'Yes, we found some wonderful chariots here. They

have gone to Cairo now'. Robert smiled as he remembered pulling Tut out of quicksand with a chariot wheel. 'Well,' said Carter, 'you had better hurry if you want to catch Harry. Tell the Sergeant on duty that I've given you all permission to go into the tomb. Keep up the painting, young lady.'

Archie was still shaking his head in amusement as they followed Pecky Callender and Harry Burton down the passageway to the burial chamber in Tut's tomb. Without even asking, by just being herself, Lucy had succeeded in getting them in. As soon as the metal gate swung open, Robert slipped inside the tomb and raced ahead. He peered through the opening that led from the antechamber to the annex and gasped in horror. It was as though the contents of the tomb had been thrown up into the air to rest wherever they landed. A harness had been strung up, reaching out into the annex. Robert figured that it was to allow the archaeologists to swing out and pluck items from the floor without disturbing anything. Robert had no time to worry about that; he had to get into the room and do it fast. He could hear the others approaching.

'Atchoo!' sneezed Harry Burton, 'I think I'm coming down with a cold.'

Robert used the harness to lower himself into the annex. He wasn't sure where to put the senet set, but he recognised the animal-shaped legs, upside down in a corner, of the set on which he had played with Tut, so he decided to reunite the two board games. Then he froze. He was ready to leave, but he could hear voices very close to the entrance to the annex.

'I'm going to experiment with taking a photograph using magnesium flash,' said Harry Burton, 'I won't really be able to see what I'm doing. Atchoo! I'll just have to point and hope for the best.'

'I'll be able to rig up some proper lighting later this afternoon. Using that flash powder always looks a little primitive to me,' said Pecky.

'True, nothing much has changed since the turn of the century. Atchoo! I've heard tell that the Germans are developing a flashbulb, but at the moment, this is the best we have.'

Archie, James and Lucy were watching. They had been hoping for a tap on the shoulder from Robert to say he had completed his mission, but it didn't come, and they realised he must still be in the annex. Harry Burton balanced a large plate-glass camera at the entrance, blocking Robert's exit. Then he held out a shallow tray mounted on a pole and poured powder from a bottle into it. He was just in the process of threading the contraption through the entrance to the annex when, 'Atchoo!' he sneezed, and the powder billowed into the room.

'Drat! Pour some more powder in, won't you, Pecky? Atchoo! I don't think this was a good idea.' Pecky poured some magnesium into the tray, Harry Burton pressed the shutter on the camera and there was a bright flash as the magnesium ignited.

'That will do. Atchoo! Come on, let's get out of here.' Harry ushered the Baxters out. Lucy and James were extremely worried about Robert as they stepped through the iron gate into the bright Egyptian sunshine, but Archie had formed a plan. Just as he got to the gate, he spoke to Pecky.

'Silly me! I've dropped my glasses. Won't be a moment, I can't read a thing without them.' Before there could be any response, he turned and headed back down the passageway.

'Uncle, I'm here. I'm coming,' whispered Robert.

Archie pretended to pick up his glasses in case Pecky was watching.

'It took me a while to climb out without damaging anything,' complained Robert, 'What's going on? First, I got covered in white powder, and then I was nearly blinded by an explosion!'

***

Robert having safely exited the tomb, the Baxters made the journey back to the Nile, before travelling to Luxor to spend their last evening at the hotel. Robert leapt into the river, fully-clothed, as everyone was worried about the explosive chemicals that covered him from head to foot. He had no desire to turn into a firework!

Meanwhile, Harry Burton was mixing chemicals to develop the photograph he had taken in the tomb. He called out from his darkroom for Howard Carter to look at the result.

'I say, Howard. What do you make of this?' The two men stared at the photograph and were astonished to see the ghostly apparition of a boy outlined in specks of white. Harry Burton had captured Robert, covered in magnesium powder, in the moments before it turned invisible. 'It must be just a trick of the light. Maybe, after I sneezed powder into the room, I didn't wait long enough for it to settle.'

'Burn it and destroy the negative,' replied Howard Carter, 'I know I encourage people to believe the curse is true, to stop tourists from bothering me or trying to sneak into the tomb, but we can't let anyone see this or we would never hear the end of it!'

CHAPTER TWENTY-ONE

After breakfast, the Baxters waited in the hotel lounge for their Uncle Archie before travelling back with Big Bessie to the lab. 'What have you got there, Lucy?' asked James, seeing his sister studying a folded piece of paper.

'Before we left the lab, I copied the hieroglyphics from our medallions. Now I'm trying to read them. It's dead annoying; I used to be able to read hieroglyphics really easily when I was back in Ancient Egypt. Now it's like dredging up the memory of a subject I learned at school years ago. It's a struggle.'

'Remembering any of my lessons from just a few weeks ago is a struggle for me,' laughed Robert.

'Anyway, I think I've done it. I was hoping for something deeply moving, but it's a bit nonsensical, really,' said Lucy, pointing to the paper. 'This one just has the letter "R", that one is "well well", the next says "you better" and the last one is "are you well?" I can play around with the order, I suppose.' Lucy tore the inscriptions into four pieces and was busying herself rearranging them on the table when Archie arrived.

'Uncle Archie, I've deciphered the hieroglyphics written on our medallions. If you arrange them correctly, they say, "R you better, are you well, well, well." It's a bit of a cruel joke because we hoped scanning them would make Robert well, but he's not!' Archie didn't answer. He stood with a perplexed expression. Then he started to hum; he raised his eyebrows and smiled.

'I've got it,' he said, 'You know me and my classic rock and pop songs! They are the lyrics from a song by Georgie Fame and Alan Price. Only the "R" isn't Robert. It's "Rosetta." Rosetta, are you better? Are you well, well, well?'

'But I came across the word Rosetta when I was researching just before we left the lab. The Rosetta Stone. It's a stela, isn't it?' said Lucy excitedly.

'You're talking a foreign language again,' complained Robert. 'If Big Bessie can't explain, you will have to.'

'Simple! A stela was a proclamation carved into a stone. If you remember, Big Bessie used to pick me up from a boundary stela in Amarna,' explained Lucy. 'Anyway, the Rosetta Stone was carved with the same thing in three different languages: in hieroglyphics, in the more common hieratic script and Ancient Greek. So, it was like cracking a code; archaeologists knew how to read Greek, so that meant they could decipher the hieroglyphics.'

'That's right, Lucy,' said Archie. 'The Rosetta Stone is in the British Museum now.'

'I don't mean to be pessimistic,' said Lucy, 'But although we hoped that putting the senet set back in the tomb would cure Robert's invisibility, I have a feeling that Big Bessie hasn't finished with us yet. Surely the Rosetta Stone is going to play a part in all of this!'

***

It all happened exactly as they feared. The warning sign about the senet game was still displayed when the Baxters returned to the lab. Archie pressed a button to confirm that they had returned it to the tomb. They all looked at where they knew Robert was standing, but there was no change - two visible Baxter children and one invisible one. Then they heard a 'ping' from Big Bessie and everyone rushed over to look at the display. James got there first.

'Eighteen with a bullet,' he read, 'What does that mean?'

'I think it's another pop reference,' replied Archie. 'It was a record in the mid-seventies. I remember the meaning being explained on the radio. It was an American disc jockey term. A bullet was a record destined for the top.'

'We've got two musical references now,' said James. 'I guess there's a connection. We can see the Rosetta Stone at any time if it's in the British Museum.'

'Why 'eighteen'?' asked Robert. 'I mean, I assume it was a chart position that was sung about, but what is the relevance to us?'

'Could it be that the Rosetta Stone was discovered in the Eighteenth Century?' asked Lucy. 'Maybe Big Bessie wants us to be there when it was first discovered, or even help it to be discovered.'

'It sounds almost like a plan,' said James.

Thirty minutes later, there was more of a plan in place.

'Rosetta, also called Rashid, is a port city way up north, in Egypt's Nile Delta,' explained Archie.' Fortunately, we know that a French officer called Pierre-François Bouchard discovered the Stone on 15th July 1799. Unfortunately, that was during the Napoleonic campaign, when England was at war with France. I think it might be too dangerous for you to go, so I'll go and investigate. As you know, as long as there is someone in the lab, they can operate Big Bessie and pull me back from wherever I am. It's a pity it doesn't work like that for you three, or else maybe I wouldn't have lost you in Ancient Egypt. You always have to come back from the same place you landed. Anyway, Lucy, you are in charge of the lab. Not that I don't trust you two boys!'

'Oh! You are very wise not to trust us, Uncle. Lucy's the boss!' agreed James.

'I'm going to arrive at the Coptic Church in Rosetta; it's been there since the sixth century, so it's easy to set the coordinates. I'm giving myself two hours in Rosetta, but I should be back in five minutes. If I am longer than ten minutes, press the button to bring me back.'

'Okay, Uncle.' Ten minutes passed, but it seemed like an hour. Lucy tried to do some more research, but she couldn't concentrate. Finally, she rushed over to the time machine, pressed a button, held her breath and crossed her fingers. To everyone's relief, Archie reappeared. His clothes were somewhat dishevelled.

'Hmmm! That didn't go quite to plan.'

'What happened, Uncle?' asked Lucy.

'I walked out of the church and was immediately surrounded by French soldiers. They could tell that I wasn't French or Egyptian, so they marched me to the military prison at gunpoint. You rescued me from the prison. That was on the day the Stone was found. I'll try a day earlier.

Same rules - give me ten minutes.' Ten minutes later, Lucy pressed the button and once again Archie arrived back in the room. This time, his clothes were in even more of a mess, not only that, he was panting and soaking wet.

'Good news and bad news. I found the building I was looking for. The Rosetta Stone was incorporated into the foundations of a fortress three hundred years ago. The bad news is that the soldiers found me again, and I had to make a dash for it. When I got to the harbour, there was nowhere else to run, so I had to dive into the sea. You got to me just in time. I could sense bullets thudding into the water all around me and, of course, that's why they caught me so quickly on my previous visit. They were still looking for me from the day before.'

'Uncle,' said James, 'I have to say that things often go wrong when you go back in time by yourself. I'm not being stupidly overconfident, but I think that if we three went, we would attract less attention.'

***

Lucy and James waited inside the church while Robert went outside to investigate. Reluctantly, their Uncle had had to agree that he stood very little chance of success by himself, so he would stay in the lab and only join them in Egypt if they were late coming back. Robert called from the door:

'All clear!'

The Baxter children stepped out into a bright, sunny, Egyptian morning and began to walk, Lucy directing the way, for she had memorised the route to Fort Julien. Robert used it as a training exercise and raced to the end of every street to check for French soldiers.

'No wonder Uncle Archie was out of breath,' said Lucy, staring at the low, squat fort guarding the last stretch of the Nile before it reached the Mediterranean Sea. 'It must be at least two miles away from the town.'

'I'll find the stone first,' said Robert, 'Then we'll figure out what we do next. You wait here, out of sight, while I go for a run.' Robert settled down to a steady jog. He was clutching a leather water bottle. Even though there had been an ample supply of lemonade and cola in the lab, he had resisted, because he wanted to be in peak condition to cope with running under the hot Egyptian sun. From Archie's description, he knew which part of the fort to head to. He slowed down and crept along quietly for the last stretch. He could see men working in a ditch at the base of the fort. Their sleeves were rolled up, they were sweating profusely, and they were speaking French.

'Mon Dieu, it's hot work!' said one. 'Fifteen more minutes, and we can stop for lunch. I need a bottle of wine and a little sleep.'

'What are we going to do with that big stone? I think we need to replace it. You can tell It's old by all that scratchy writing. How shall we get it out? I can't be bothered to chisel around it and prise it out.'

'I shall take my trusty sledgehammer to it, but let's wait until after lunch.'

'We mustn't be late back. Lieutenant Bouchard is going to be inspecting our work this afternoon.'

'All the more reason to knock off early. Come on, let's go.' Before the soldiers had taken a single step, Robert was already running at full pelt back to his brother and sister.

It didn't take long for the children to arrive at the reinforced doors to Fort Julien.

'Now what? How do we get in?' asked James.

'Look!' cried Robert. He pointed, which, as he was invisible, was pretty pointless. 'Behind you!' Lucy and James turned and saw a horse and cart approaching. 'Just play in the sand, draw pictures or something like a couple of kids. I'm sure you'll be ignored. Then see if you can climb on the back of the cart.' This was just the sort of challenge Robert loved.

The horse and cart stopped outside the fort, and the driver climbed down and rapped on the door with the end of his whip. Robert quickly inspected the cart but was disappointed. The waggon had low sides and was stacked with barrels marked 'vin'. There was absolutely nowhere to hide. Robert rushed back to Lucy and James, who were waiting in the expectation of hitching a ride.

'It's no good. I'll follow it in and see if I can open the door from the inside. Stay close.' Robert rushed back. The Arab driver was having a conversation through an inspection hatch with the guard.

'How much wine can one garrison drink?' he laughed. 'I don't know how you lot stay alert.'

'Don't you worry about that,' replied the guard as he swung open the door to let the horse and cart through. 'It's in our culture.' The horse and cart trundled on through the courtyard. Robert watched the guard turn a key in a large padlock and slot an iron bar into place to secure the door before retreating to a lean-to hut. There wasn't any glass in its window, but it was probably still hot and stuffy inside. Robert watched the guard take a quick, furtive drink from a bottle of wine hidden under a sack, pull up a chair and settle down for a little nap. Robert could see the key on a table. He worked his top half through the window and reached for it. With a little more wriggling and stretching, he managed to grasp it. He didn't have to wait for the key to turn invisible because the guard's eyes were closed. Just as he was letting his brother and sister in, Robert heard the sound of the horse and cart returning.

'Quick! Hide behind those crates; I've got to return the key.' When he got back to the hut, the guard was reluctantly hauling himself out of his chair, his slumbers disturbed by the approaching waggon.

'Agh! Where is that key?' he muttered. He checked under the table. He wasn't to know that an invisible key had just been placed on it. By the time he straightened up, it was visible again. 'There it is, exactly where I left it. Maybe that Arab has a point; I must cut down on the wine.' Robert smiled and then raced back to where James and Lucy were hiding. They were in!

A group of soldiers entered the courtyard. James turned to Lucy:

'My turn now; follow my lead, Lucy.' He strode out into the centre of the courtyard to talk to the soldiers.

'Excuse me, would you gentlemen be kind enough to point us in the direction of Lieutenant Bouchard's office? We have a message for him,' he said confidently. The soldiers were bemused. They had never seen children in the fort before. One of them glanced over to the doors. He could see they were shut, so presumably, the pair had permission to be here. They looked European, and the boy spoke perfect French.

'Give me your message, and I will pass it on to him.'

'No, thank you kindly; we need to speak to him in person,' replied James.

'He is a busy man.'

'I am sure you all have things you should be doing, Sir. Kindly give me the information I have requested and I won't keep you any longer,' said James firmly.

'Oh, very well. It's in that round section of the fort, at the top,' said the soldier, pointing. James thanked him and the men went on their way, teasing the one who had spoken for being bossed about by a child.

'Probably an officer's kid,' he grumbled, 'It won't do to make enemies - I might end up on permanent guard duty patrolling the desert!'

'My turn now,' said Lucy as they knocked on the Lieutenant's door. She was nervous, but she was the only one who had researched him before they came, so she knew she was best equipped to take the initiative.

'Enter.' Lieutenant Bouchard looked up from his papers in surprise when he saw Lucy and James.

'Excuse me,' said Lucy politely, 'We apologise for disturbing you, but we have some urgent news. It is something that could change your life forever.'

'Really?' replied Bouchard in a dismissive tone that suggested he didn't believe a word of it.

'Honestly. We believe that you are the most deserving person to have this opportunity.'

'And how do you come to that conclusion?'

'First of all, you have an interest in Egyptian antiquities.'

'That's true. When I arrived in this country, my first job involved investigating Egyptian crafts and techniques.'

'And what I am about to tell you will bring you world renown. What better way to climb the ranks in the army? I predict that within fifteen years, you will be awarded the Order of the Légion d'Honneur.' It was an easy prediction for Lucy to make because she knew it would happen in July 1814. The Lieutenant was curious now.

'Just imagine, you will be able to bring your wife over to Egypt,' continued Lucy.

'How did you know I was married?' Lucy feared she had gone too far. She remembered he had married only three months earlier.

'Oh,' she said hastily, I just knew a man as handsome as you was bound to be married. All I ask, Sir, is just fifteen minutes of your time. I want you to look at something, an Egyptian antiquity that will change the course of history. There will be nothing to stem the tide of fame that will come your way. You will be in the history books forever. You deserve it. '

'By God, I do deserve it,' shouted Bouchard, leaping to his feet. Show me this thing.'

Five minutes later, they were outside the fort once more. The guard had been puzzled about how the children had got inside in the first place, but he decided not to pursue the matter. He resolved to try a week without wine, or maybe the rest of the day...or at any rate the rest of the working day.

'First of all, I do not want anyone to know about our conversation,' said Lucy, 'You must get all the credit. Let me tell you about what you are looking at. Do you see that stone built into the wall? It's a stela. The inscription on it is written in three different languages. No one has been able to read hieroglyphics for thousands of years, but now, by comparing the hieroglyphics with the Greek writing, historians will be able to decipher their meaning.'

'Prepare to be famous,' piped up James, feeling very envious. He would have loved to be famous. The Lieutenant jumped into the ditch and ran his hands over the Rosetta Stone. Robert whispered urgently:

'Come on you two. Our work here is done. Let's get back to the church.' On the way the Baxters passed the soldiers who had been working in the trench and who were now hurrying back from their long lunch break. One of them was carrying a sledgehammer. Without the intervention of Big Bessie and the Baxters, the Rosetta Stone would have been smashed to pieces.

'We're a little late,' said Lucy in a worried voice as they hurried to the church. The road had been relatively quiet earlier, but now it was beginning to fill with Egyptians setting up an evening market and soldiers who, although they ignored James and Lucy, seemed to be searching for something.

'I call that a real team effort,' said James cheerily, 'Oh look, there's the fourth member of the team.' On the steps of the church stood Uncle Archie. His arms were outstretched and he had a broad smile. How often had they seen him just like that? From behind them came a shout in French.

'There he is!' They turned their heads to see a soldier raise a musket to his shoulder and take aim. Lucy screamed as there was a loud crack and a puff of smoke. She turned back towards her Uncle and began to run. He lay spreadeagled on the steps, one hand clutching his chest where the bullet had pierced his jacket.

'Uncle! Uncle!' she cried, but there was no response.

'Lucy,' urged Robert, 'We have to go. We've only got a couple of minutes for Big Bessie to collect us, otherwise we will get stuck here.'

'But we can't leave him here,' she wailed.

'We have to, for now,' said Robert, 'But don't worry, when we get back to the lab, we can reprogramme Big Bessie to collect him.'

CHAPTER TWENTY-TWO

Despite her trembling hands and uncontrollable sobs, Lucy reprogrammed Big Bessie faster than she had ever done before. She pressed the 'start' button, and she and her brothers stood by the glass screen to wait for their uncle. Lucy was still crying. James bit his lip, he had fears, but he didn't voice them. What if Big Bessie didn't work on dead people? Suddenly, lights flashed and then there was their uncle lying flat on the floor. As they rushed to him, they heard him groan.

'He's still alive!' shouted Robert. They gathered around him.

'Ohhh! I think I hit my head on the church step. I must have passed out.'

'It's worse than that,' said Lucy gently, 'You've been shot.'

'Quick, let's check the wound,' said Robert, unbuttoning Archie's jacket and shirt.

'Ohhh! my chest hurts!' groaned Archie.

'Whaaaat?' exclaimed Robert. He had peeled his uncle's clothes back and was staring at a sheet of iron fastened to Archie's body with leather straps. Above his heart, lodged in the crude breastplate, was a lead bullet. It had severely dented the metal, but it hadn't pierced it. Archie raised himself to his elbows and peered down at his chest.

'When I left the lab, this was a fairly modern bulletproof vest. It converted to something rather basic, but it appears to have done the job. Oooh! It's sore, though. I'll have a nasty bruise.'

'Stay there, Uncle. I had better do some tests to see if you have concussion,' said Robert. His First Aid training was getting some more use. First a near-drowned brother and now a nearly-shot uncle!

'I need a cup of tea,' said Lucy, 'I'm sure we all do.'

Later, with Archie given the all-clear by Robert, they sat around the table nursing cups of tea. They were all very shaken by their ordeal.

'Actually, there was a fine song by The Beatles called "Doctor Robert." I'll think of this moment when I hear it again,' said Archie.

'I don't understand what we are supposed to do next,' said Lucy, worriedly. 'We've scanned the medallions, taken the senet board game back and saved the Rosetta Stone from being smashed up. What more can we do?' No one had an answer. Robert drummed his fingers on the table as if to say, 'I'm here, I'm still invisible, but I'm here.' Archie winced and rubbed the bruise on his chest. James rolled the bullet around on the table; he had prised it out of Archie's bulletproof vest. Were the Baxters defeated?

'What do you want me to do with this, Uncle?' James asked, 'Do you have a display case in the museum for eighteenth-century bullets?'

'Eighteenth-century bullets,' repeated Lucy, emphasising each word.

'Eighteen with a bullet!' shouted all four Baxters. A moment's pause...then several moments of activity: flashing lights, a 'ping' from Big Bessie's scanner, then the bullet was registered into the museum's catalogue and Robert entered the world of visible people.

'Goodness, Robert!' exclaimed Lucy, 'You might have made an effort! You look like you've been dragged through a hedge backwards!' Robert was filthy, his clothes were ripped and torn and his hair was tangled. It was a long time since it had seen a comb!

'I've been busy,' he protested. 'I've been lost in a sand storm, fought against a crocodile, swum in the Aswan Dam, crawled through a tomb, and done a lot of running. Not to mention travelling to the Egyptian afterlife. Personal hygiene wasn't at the top of my list.'

'Well done, all you Baxters,' said Archie. 'It's time for a celebration. I'll download some music. We have to have "Rosetta" by Alan Price and Georgie Fame and "Eighteen with a bullet" by Pete Wingfield. And of course "Doctor Robert" by the Beatles.'

'And this,' said James, doing his funny sideways walk, 'It's "Walk like an Egyptian" by The Bangles. I'll order the pizza, shall I?'

'Ermmm,' Robert was torn; he was trying to eat healthily, 'Oh, why not? It's a party. Italy is in the Med, isn't it, so surely pizza counts as part of a healthy Mediterranean diet!'

***

At first, everyone was astonished when James did not audition for the leading role in the School production of "Joseph and the Amazing Technicolor Dreamcoat". Robert and Lucy were not surprised, though, because when he performed on stage as Pharaoh, the audience went wild. They were particularly impressed with the range of tricks he executed with a walking stick; at various times, it was like a martial arts staff, a pop singer's microphone stand, or a cane in a 1930s Hollywood tap-dancing routine. Pure genius!

***

After a momentary lapse in the lab party, when he over-indulged on pizza, Robert developed amazing powers of self-discipline and stuck to a true Mediterranian diet. Out too went the fizzy drinks; Robert's enforced stay in Ancient Egypt meant that he now valued plain water. Speaking of water, Robert enjoyed the sensation of swimming in the school pool without worrying about whether a crocodile was about to snap at his heels. The results of his new training regime were clear to see when he mounted the podium at the school's sports day and held his winner's medal aloft. No one heard him when he whispered thanks to the boy king, Tutankhamun, and wished him well in the afterlife.

***

Henri Pastiche scowled as he sat in the waiting room. His train was late. He was now Lucy's 'ex' art teacher. The school had not renewed his contract; he had upset too many people. His mood wasn't improved when, leafing through an Arts and Craft magazine, he spotted a feature on Lucy Baxter, who had submitted an entry, against his advice, to a national Art competition and come first. She had submitted a large, decorated pot, which she said had been inspired by the artist Grayson Perry and which featured scenes of Egyptian life. She explained that the hieroglyphics around the rim spelt Nefertiti, Life, Prosperity, Health. She added that Nefertiti was a truly inspirational queen.

***

Archie placed the bullet in a display case in the museum. Probably no one else would notice it; visitors would be more interested in the antique firearms on show. However, whenever Archie saw it, he would always be reminded that, although the bullet had nearly killed him, it had saved Robert Baxter.

***

Upstairs, in the kitchen, a new member of the Baxter household waited patiently. Her name was Neferkitty, but everyone just called her Kitty, and she crouched with her nose close to a hole in the skirting board, waiting to pounce. Her whiskers twitched - she could definitely smell mouse! She was right. A few feet away, under the floorboards, was a very frightened and hungry mouse. He had come to a decision. After a few near misses with the terrifying creature that stalked his every move, he realised it wasn't safe to live in this house anymore. It was time to travel to pastures new.

A NOTE FROM THE AUTHOR

History inspires me, but as with all the books in the Stuck series, this is not a history textbook. I happily moved the dates of events and invented characters to suit the story. If you are interested in some of the history of Egypt and would like to know about examples of where I have used artistic licence, read on.

I refer frequently to Luxor being the ancient city of Thebes. The Egyptians wouldn't have called it Thebes (that was what the ancient Greeks called this city) but would probably have referred to it as Waset.

Most people know about the discovery of Tutankhamun's tomb in 1922. There are differing opinions as to whether Howard Carter, Lord Carnarvon and his daughter Evelyn paid a secret visit to the tomb. I doubt we will ever know for certain. Howard Carter did not break into the burial chamber until February 17th 1923. In my story, Robert beats him to it, in November 1922!

The Egyptians loved to design an artefact that would contain another, which in turn would contain another, etc. Tutankhamun's canopic chest, described in the story, was actually within a large, gilded, wooden shrine. However, I decided it would give Robert too much to do if he had to tackle this too. If he had taken the stoppers off the canopic chest, he would have discovered they contained miniature sarcophagi, copies of Tutankhamun's coffin. He would have made the delightful discovery of three-thousand-year-old entrails inside them!

Mary Chubb and her team existed, and I enjoyed reading her autobiography, "Nefertiti Lived Here." However, her first expedition to Egypt was in 1930, so I moved it back to 1922. Some of the events I drew on did happen, like discovering the brightly-painted lintel in the house of Hatiay, an Overseer of Works. The hoard of 'stolen' treasure was found in a different, smaller house, so I invented a corrupt official, Nebkef, to be the owner of the loot. No one knows what happened to him and why he didn't return to collect it, but I know that the city suffered from outbreaks of the plague, so by inflicting the disease on him I gave Lucy an empty house in which to bury her pot.
I compressed the timespan of various events that concern the Pharaoh to make them all fit within the story. The

opening of the new Gem Pa Aten temple complex in Karnak happened in the first few years of the Pharaoh's reign. It was from here, in the second year of his reign, that Amenhotep 1V probably gave the speech to the senior courtiers where he revealed the supremacy of the sun god, Aten. Fragments of this speech have survived. Amenhotep founded the new city in year four of his reign, although he didn't return to live there for another year. He changed his name to Akhenaten in regnal year five. The Festival of Tribute described in the story took place in 1351 BCE, year twelve of his reign.

The period of Ancient Egypt described in the book is famous for a new artistic style, referred to now as "The Amarna Style." Artists began to draw the human figure in an exaggerated and distorted fashion. In my story, this evolved from a cartoon that Lucy drew. Near the end of the book Lucy leaves a message for Thutmose, a sculptor about to begin a commission of Nefertiti. If you search on the internet, the beautiful bust he made of Nefertiti will probably be the first image you see.

We don't know what happened to Nefertiti. She eventually went on to have at least six daughters. One of them, Ankhesenamun, became Tutankhamun's young wife. Nefertiti may even have ruled as Pharaoh herself after her husband's death, using the name Neferneferuaten. Maybe one day the mystery will be solved.

There was a High Priest Maya at the Temple of Amun during the time my story is set but everything I have written about him - apart from the wealth of the temple, which rivalled that of the Pharaoh - is fiction. Potasimto was an Egyptian General who fought against the Nubians some 300 years later. I chose him to appear in my story purely because I liked his name.

Why did Robert and James think that the Ramses Temple at Abu Simbel had been stolen? It wasn't stolen; they had arrived when it was in the process of being moved. The creation of the Aswan Dam in the 1960s would have meant that many ancient monuments would be submerged, so Unesco embarked on its first-ever collaborative international rescue effort. In an amazing feat of engineering, they cut the temple up into 16,000 precise blocks and moved it to higher ground.

Gamal Abdel Nasser was President of Egypt from 1956-1970 and was born in the village of Beni Murr, where his father ran a post office. However, he was sent to live with his uncle, Khali Hussein, in Cairo, not Luxor. This happened two years later than my story is set. Politically, 1922 was a time of unrest and there were protests as the Egyptians sought independence from Britain.

I would like to draw your attention to a great podcast called "The History of Egypt Podcast" www.egyptianhistorypodcast.com. It's written and narrated by Dominic Perry. As well as an insightful and detailed exploration of Ancient Egypt (as I write there are around 200 episodes), it contains interviews with several eminent archaeologists. I learned so much from these podcasts - thank you, Dominic, may the sun disc shine forever on your house.

Finally, I would like to thank Rachel Laurence for the tremendous contribution she has made to all my books. I value her analytical mind, her command of the English language and the fact that she truly loves the Baxter family, ensuring the books are ready for print. As she narrates the 'Stuck' audiobooks too, they are also ready for your ears. If anyone deserves a gigantic stela carved into the side of a cliff, it's Rachel!

Would you like to read more books in this series?

 You can order the 'Stuck' series from Amazon by visiting this page on my website (they are all stand-alone books): www.stuckdave.co.uk/blink

You can also join my mailing list and find information about upcoming publications and have the opportunity to win free stuff! I would love it if you followed me on Instagram, too: @stuckdavewrites

Finally, I would really appreciate it if you could write a review on Amazon of my book. Even if you did not buy this book yourself from Amazon, you should still be able to post a review there.

Printed in Great Britain
by Amazon

21514534R00130